Genevieve's Journey

Genevieve's Journey

Valerie Foote

Charleston, SC
www.PalmettoPublishing.com

Genevieve's Journey

First Edition

Paperback ISBN: 978-1-63837-412-1

*This book is dedicated to my parents
who inspired my love of books,
my cousin Carol for all her guidance,
and
Christopher, my Italian monk.*

Contents

G enevieve awoke with a start, wondering where she was. Her body was flooded with warmth despite the cold night. She nestled closer to the embrace of the body next to her. Here she was lying in the arms of a young man she had just met, who knew nothing about her secret. Who was this good man? He was so unlike her brutal husband. Was she safe at last, finally out of her husband's grasp? With no family or friends left to help her, this place was her only alternative. But how had she gotten to this point in her short life?

PART ONE:
Childhood: France, Late 1400's

Chapter One

G enevieve was quite young when her mother died. It was a typical case of complications at childbirth where both the mother and child died. They were buried in the churchyard even though the baby had not survived long enough to be baptized. Pere LeMaitre was a kindly priest and allowed such a burial. He was a priest who knew the meaning of Christian charity. Pere LeMaitre was well loved by his flock and would prove his kindness to Genevieve later in her life.

All that Genevieve remembered about her mother was the brilliant color of her hair, a unique auburn color that stood out in a crowd. Her mother would unbind her hair at night and brush it till it glistened. Often her father would nestle his head in her long locks. Then she would braid it again in a long plait for the night. Genevieve remembered wishing her mother would wear it loose during the day so she could see the sunlight play on its strands.

Genevieve was also reminded of her mother every spring when the lilacs were in bloom. They were her mother's favorite flower and she would pick them by the handfuls to bring into their cottage, placing them in a vase on their table. The whole room was filled with their sweet scent and her mother would periodically bury her nose in the delicate blossoms.

As the years passed, Genevieve grew more and more like her mother, with the same delicate features, unusual green eyes and glorious auburn hair. But one day some of the village children teased her, pulling her hair and accusing her of being the devil's offspring. This terrified her because she knew what was done to women accused of consorting with the devil and practicing witchcraft. Crying, she screamed:

"I am not the devil's child! I am not! My hair is just like my mother's and you know she was a good woman, a healer and a devoted wife! Stop this right now!"

Just then Pere LeMaitre appeared, much to Genevieve's relief. She trusted he knew she was not the devil's child.

"My children, my children! What is happening here? Are you teasing my friend about her beautiful hair? This must stop. Her hair in all its beauty is a gift from God, as well as a gift from her mother, a rare gift and to be treasured! You must not accuse and tease. You are all still babes, young and pure in the eyes of God, and so you must believe in and treasure the innocence and goodness of each other."

The children looked chagrined and soon were apologizing to Genevieve, much to her relief. She quickly ran up and embraced Pere LeMaitre in thanks for his timely appearance and kind words. He knelt down and wiped her eyes and nose with a rough cloth, rough like the texture of his robe. She was surprised that such a gentle soul should be clothed in such roughness. None-the-less, she buried her face in his shoulder and gave a last gulp of sorrow followed by a long sigh of contentment.

"You are a special princess, my dear Genevieve. Be sure to remember that! Now go play with your friends," he concluded.

"Yes, Pere LeMaitre, thank you!" She gave him a quick curtsy as she had been taught to do as a sign of respect and scurried off.

Genevieve's father was a kind man and a gifted metal worker who was known far and wide for his delicate creations of jewelry.

His biggest patron was the Viscount Bruneau whose estates bordered the tiny village where Genevieve lived. She often played on his estate, hunting for mushrooms in his forests and racing among the tall sheaves of wheat. She was eight years old when she finally met Delphine, the viscount's daughter.

The day came when her father asked her to deliver a piece of jewelry to the viscount, a pair of earrings, with beautiful light blue stones set in a filigree of gold.

"Genevieve, I need you to help me today. I am behind in my commission for the Duke, yet I must get these earrings to the viscount for his daughter's birthday celebration. I simply do not have the time and I think you are responsible enough to do this errand for me. Would you do it? But remember, do not give the package to anyone but the viscount. That is our arrangement. We don't dare risk having something of such value misplaced, lost or even stolen."

"Yes, Papa."

Genevieve felt honored to be trusted by her father with such an important mission. With the utmost care, Genevieve placed the carefully wrapped piece of jewelry in her basket, and with her best clothes on and her hair neatly brushed, she started the long walk across the estate lands to the viscount's grand chateau.

When she arrived a half hour later, she was confronted with which door to approach: the servant's entrance or the front door. She felt sure that her father's marvelous gift deserved to be presented at the front door. Boldly, she knocked as loudly as she could and waited. Soon she heard locks being unfastened and the heavy door creaking open. A servant peered out and looked in surprise at Genevieve.

"What on earth are you doing at our door, young lady? Be gone with you!"

"But I come from the artisan Bertrand with a gift for the young mistress! And I have sworn to my father to deliver it in person, just as he does."

She had such a determined tone in her voice and expression on her face that the doorman smiled and opened the door.

"Oh, you are here on the behalf of Artisan Bertrand! And why have you been chosen as his envoy?" asked the doorman kindly.

"I am his only child and I am almost nine years old, old enough to help my father!" Genevieve said proudly.

"Very well, your ladyship, follow me," said the doorman with a chuckle.

Genevieve had never been inside such a huge building. On all the walls hung paintings and tapestries. Down the long hall and up the stairs she went, following closely behind lest she get lost. They finally reached an open hall with walls painted in white, covered with paintings and armament. Soft colorful carpets lay on the wooden floors. A huge fireplace dominated the room and many chairs and tables were placed around the room. Genevieve could not take her eyes off of her surroundings, until a voice boomed out announcing her arrival as the daughter of Artisan Bertrand. Coming to her senses, she quickly dropped a curtsy and respectfully lowered her head.

"Well, come here, my child, and show us what you have brought," said the viscount.

It was then that Genevieve looked at the three people in the room: the viscount, his wife and their daughter. A tiny white puppy played at their feet. Genevieve was fascinated by the daughter who was probably close to her age, and here she was receiving a gift fit for a queen, Genevieve thought.

The girl appeared to be frail, not robust and energetic like Genevieve, but rather pale and delicate, with stringy blonde hair and a slight overbite, though she did have lovely blue eyes.

Genevieve thought of her own luxurious auburn hair and sparkling green eyes, and her heart went out to the little girl. Her thoughts were interrupted when the viscount spoke.

"Come child, let me look at you. Why, you look so like your mother whom I remember well. She came here to help my wife with my daughter when she was first born. They were sickly at the time and your mother had a gift with herbs and remedies which I'm sure saved their lives. We never forgot her kindness and healing touch. I was very sorry to hear that she had died soon after giving birth to your sister."

During this remembrance, Genevieve had a chance to observe the viscount and note his dissimilarity to his daughter. Brown haired and blue eyed with a ruddy complexion, what she noticed most was his red nose and slightly bloodshot eyes. She curtsied again and carefully began to hand the basket to the viscount.

He stopped her and said:

"Please, it is a gift for my daughter, Delphine. You must give it to her. After all, it is her ninth birthday and I promised her a gift fit for a princess."

So they were the same age, Genevieve thought. Little did she know what an important person the girl Delphine would be in her life.

As Genevieve turned, she got a glimpse of his wife who was lounging in a chair by a fire even though it was a warm day. Ah, that was where Delphine got her looks: the pale white skin, blonde hair, light blue eyes and the slight overbite. She was a prettier but less healthy version of her daughter but still no beauty. As well, it was obvious that she was with child. Quickly, Genevieve curtsied in her direction and then turned to Delphine, holding out her basket.

"Papa, another gift for me?! You are too kind. I thought the puppy was my special gift but now I am to receive a real lady's gift! Quick, let me see!"

Delphine grabbed the package from the basket and hastily tore open the wrapping. Her mouth dropped open when she saw the delicate earrings. She held them up to the light, gasping with pleasure. Genevieve pulled a mirror from out of the basket. The mirror was her father's prize possession and been a favorite of her mother's. She held up the mirror for Delphine, who carefully placed the earrings up to her earlobes and tossed her head from side to side, smiling with pleasure.

"Come darling," said her mother. "Let me put them in your ears for you. Then you can really see how beautiful they are."

When her mother was done, she raced to hug her father.

"Papa, I love them, they are so pretty! Thank you so much! I love them just as much as my puppy," Delphine exclaimed.

Just then several servants arrived with trays of food. Genevieve realized it was time for luncheon and her stomach growled.

"Join us for the meal before you return home, Genevieve. And you must give your father our great thanks and admiration for his work. He is a true artist!"

"Thank you kindly. I would be very grateful for a bite to eat before I start on my way home."

The meal consisted of cold meat, bread, a soft cheese and cider to drink. The cheese was a treat. She was only used to hard cheese. But best of all, after the meal, each of them received an orange! Genevieve had had an orange only once, one special Christmas and she knew they were not grown locally but were brought from the warmer countries in the south so she knew what a special treat this was.

"Sir, could I take my orange home with me to share with my papa? It is a rare treat!" she queried.

"No, you may not!" he responded much to her surprise. But then she saw the broad smile on his face as he held out another orange for her. "Take this one to your father and eat yours now with us."

After the meal, Delphine played with her puppy and introduced the little snowball of a pup to Genevieve. He was the epitome of adorable and Genevieve envied Delphine her little pet.

"What is his name?" she asked.

"I don't know. I have not decided yet. Will you help me?" Delphine replied.

Genevieve scrutinized the little pup and held him up to look at his face, hoping for some inspiration. He wriggled in her grasp and licked her face.

"He has a lot of spirit, this little beast!" she said.

"Spirit! I like that as a name! He is white as a ghost or spirit and as lively as can be.

Perfect!" Delphine exclaimed.

After the meal, Genevieve excused herself and walked home full of thoughts about the day's events.

Chapter Two

One day her father sent her out into the forest on the chateau grounds to look for edible mushrooms. She was well versed in avoiding the poisonous ones: Avenging Angels, elegant and white, looking like parasols. She was looking for Morals and the lovely fluted orange Chanterelles. Her basket was almost full when she heard whimpering in the distance. Was an animal caught in one of those awful traps that the hunters put out when poaching in the Viscount's forest? She hoped she would be able to save the creature without being bitten. Would she be brave enough?

She turned a bend in the woods and there she found Spirit, huddled and shaking in a hole at the base of a large tree. Spirit! He must have escaped from his enclosure and become lost in the woods. Putting her basket to the side, Genevieve slowly squatted down to his level and gently called his name in a soothing voice. Inch by inch, the dog emerged from the hole and sidled up to Genevieve, looking hopefully up into her face. She carefully picked him up in her arms and he licked her face.

"I must take you back right away, you poor baby. How long have you been out here? I hope not overnight. If so, you must be cold and famished. Come, Delphine must be worried sick about you!"

Genevieve continued talking in a soothing tone to Spirit as she carried him to the chateau. As if knowing he was being helped,

Spirit rested quietly in her arms, giving her the occasional wet kiss. It was lucky he was such a small dog, as Genevieve had a long way to carry him.

Finally, she arrived at the chateau fields breathless. Three men were searching in the fields calling Spirit's name.

"He's here!" she shouted and the men converged on her. They took Spirit from her and he wiggled and protested.

"Here, you come with us and carry the dog. He seems happier in your arms."

She followed the men back to the chateau to the yard they had fenced off for Spirit. Delphine sat disconsolately by Spirit's little dog house crying.

"He's here! He's here," the men called out as they approached. Delphine jumped up clapping her hand with a beaming smile across her tear-stained face.

"Spirit, ma petit chou, my sweet! Let me hold you. Are you alright? Are you hungry? Tired? Scared? My poor little baby."

Delphine cooed as she hugged him tightly to her smothering him in kisses. Spirit wriggled in delight and joy at being returned to his mistress. Delphine finally took a break from her adoration to look up and thank Genevieve. She dismissed the men and asked Genevieve to stay. Genevieve thought about her basket of mushrooms and said she must be leaving but quickly changed her mind when she saw the hugely disappointed look on Delphine's face.

"I'm sure my Papa will want to reward you! You must tell me all about how and where you found Spirit, and if he was scared, poor thing!" Delphine prattled on.

Genevieve explained how she had come upon Spirit and pretty soon the two girls were chatting and laughing and playing with Spirit, throwing a ball and running about as he chased them.

Once again, Genevieve was invited to the mid-day meal and thanked by Delphine's parents. Her already pale mother looked even paler, Genevieve though, and looked exhausted.

"Mama is going to have another baby! At last, I will have a brother or sister!" Delphine explained before her parents could reprimand her for discussing such a private matter with an outsider.

"How wonderful!" Genevieve offered.

After the meal, Delphine tugged on her father's shirt and whispered something in his ear. "Please, Papa, please!"

"Genevieve, Delphine wonders if you would like to stay the afternoon to play with her? You would be most welcome," he asked her.

"Oh, I would love to but my father is expecting me back with a basket of mushrooms that I left in the woods." Genevieve said in genuine disappointment.

"Of course, I understand. We wouldn't want him to worry. Could you come tomorrow on Sunday after church?" he asked.

"Yes, I would love to! I will be in church tomorrow. I could come directly."

"Why don't you just join us in our carriage after the service. We can all ride back to the chateau together," the viscount said.

"Oh, I'd love that. I have never driven in a carriage before!" Genevieve exclaimed.

The viscount laughed kindly at her enthusiasm. After the final arrangements were made, they said their last thank yous and goodbyes and Genevieve set off on her way as Delphine waved from Spirit's enclosure.

The next day being Sunday, the Lord's day, Genevieve and her father put on their best clothes and walked to the local church. It was a lovely spring morning, the sun shining and the flowers blooming. Genevieve held her father's hand as they strolled along. The church was in the center of the village. Because of the viscount, the church was bigger than the average church, made out of lovely warm colored stone with elegant arches and a tall spire where the bell was ringing. But the real glory of the church was its stain glass window! The viscount had insisted on this and, of course, donated the money. The confessional booth was carved out of wood with intricate designs and the baptismal font was made of marble all also paid for by the viscount. Pere LeMaitre, the priest, was very proud of his elegant church and supremely proud of the stain glass window. He knew it was a sin on his part to harbor such pride in worldly objects, but he couldn't help himself.

Genevieve loved coming to church on sunny days. She would always pause in the colored light that the stain glass window cast upon the stones. But today she was too excited to think about the colorful light and sat through the long service impatiently. Though she liked the serious sound of the Latin mass, she was most intrigued by the communion of which her father partook. She knew she would soon have her first communion and then the mystery would be over. The blood and body of Christ: this concept perplexed and somewhat disturbed her. Why would one want to eat the body and drink the blood of someone. Was this to have God inside of you, to be part of you? Her father had once told her that Christ had said it should be done in remembrance of him. Eating a human being seemed a strange way to remember someone. She had mentioned this to Pere LeMaitre in her monthly instruction at the church and he had not known how to respond to her. He said some mysteries were best left alone. So part of her was fascinated and eager for communion and part of her dreaded it.

The service seemed to go on for an eternity today. She kept glancing up to the viscount's box at the front and side of the altar. The choir boys were in the box across from them. One time when Genevieve looked at the viscount's box, Delphine turned and seeing her, smiled broadly. This added to Genevieve's excitement. She had a new friend who didn't seem to think she was strange or teased her because of the color of her hair.

After the general melee at the end of the service, Genevieve sought out Delphine eagerly. When Delphine saw her, she grabbed her hand and they ran off to the carriage to await the viscount as he greeted the priest and then helped his ailing wife along.

Genevieve had never been so close to such a beautiful horse. Its brown color was the color of chestnuts and just as shiny. It moved its hooves in vague impatience and lowered its head to be stroked by the girls.

"What is its name?" asked Genevieve.

"Name? I don't think he has a name. He's a working animal you know, not a pet."

"Still, they are animals and have feelings. He should have a name!" Genevieve responded.

"Well, I guess that is alright. But what should we call him?"

"That's easy, Chestnut! He's just the color of a chestnut!"

"Chestnut...I like that. He will be Chestnut from now on."

As if recognizing his new name, he proudly raised his head.

By now the viscount and his wife had made it to the carriage. Genevieve saw that his wife's face was paler than usual and there were beads of sweat on her brow, and she was holding her belly. The viscount lifted her into the carriage and called to the girls to hurry up and get in. He sounded worried and the viscountess groaned at every bump in the road. The viscount held her hand and spoke soothingly to her.

Instead of this being an exciting trip for Genevieve, it proved worrisome. Delphine seemed oblivious to her mother's discomfort. Perhaps she was used it, Genevieve mused. Delphine prattled on about the horse and his new name and what fun she and Genevieve were going to have back at the chateau.

"That's nice, dear," the viscountess mumbled, as she continued to hold her belly and groan at each bump. The viscount was mopping her brow and continued to hold her hand. She periodically squeezed his hand, whether it was from pain or comfort, Genevieve couldn't tell.

Back at the Chateau, the viscountess was ushered upstairs to her bed chamber and the children were left to their own devices. First, they went to visit Spirit in his big grassy enclosure and Delphine decided to bring him up to her bedchamber. Careful lest she get lost in the chateau, Genevieve followed closely behind in the dark corridors until they arrived at a charmingly painted door. It had a light blue background on which were painted fluffy white clouds. It felt as if they were entering the sky.

Once inside her bed chamber, Delphine released Spirit who had been wriggling and whining. He immediately attacked a pillow that was lying on the floor and then settled down on it. Delphine made her way to a chest at the foot of her four-poster bed. It was filled with dolls and doll clothes. She pulled out one doll after the other, introducing them by name. Genevieve marveled that the carved wooden dolls had movable joints in their arms and legs. Some were cloth dolls with their facial features stitched on in the sweetest expressions.

"This is Antoinette and she is a little vain because she is porcelain and the prettiest one." She then pulled a wooden doll from the chest and tossed it aside without an introduction.

"Who is this doll?" asked Genevieve as she picked up the doll tenderly.

"That's Caroline, but she has such a sour expression on her face. Look at her scowl," Delphine replied and then went on. "Which doll would you like to play with?"

Something about Caroline's unhappy expression appealed to Genevieve. She had character and it wasn't her fault, she thought. She looked like she was having a bad time and felt neglected and unloved. Genevieve felt sorry for the doll and held it to her.

"I think I'll play with Caroline...if you don't mind. I think she might just be lonely. I bet my father could repaint the expression on her face to make her happier."

"Well really, Genevieve, you are a funny girl. First you give a horse a name and now you pick the ugliest doll. Since you like her so much, you might as well have her for keeps."

Genevieve was overcome with joy at the thought of having such a doll and a gift from Delphine. Would her father allow her to accept such a gift? After all, she did have her beloved rag doll Henrietta, but Caroline might be company for her. Plus, Caroline wore a lovely burgundy velvet dress with white lace! It must have cost a fortune.

"Where did Caroline get this lovely gown?" asked Genevieve.

"Oh, it was made from the scraps of my Christmas dress. Every time the dressmaker comes, she makes my dollies dresses with the left-over material. Look."

Delphine began to pull doll dresses out of the chest and placed them on the floor.

"You can take another gown if you want. Every doll should have clothes for her to be changed into."

Genevieve looked at the gowns in admiration. What fine needlework! She settled on a forest green dress with gold trim. It was so elegant and beautiful, she thought. She was still marveling at her good fortune when a maid rushed into the room crying.

"Delphine, quick, you must come right now. Your mother, her time has come. The baby is coming and two months early at that! You must hurry, she is calling for you!"

The sadness and urgency in her tone let Genevieve know that something was seriously wrong with Delphine's mother. Delphine had dropped everything and ran past the maid who followed in her footsteps.

Genevieve was left all alone in the strange house and she knew she had to find her own way out. Slowly and carefully, she packed away all the dresses and dolls. Under the circumstances, she felt it would be wrong to take the doll. She gave Caroline a wistful kiss and placed her last in the chest.

After a few wrong turns, she found herself in the kitchen and left by its door. The beautiful sunny day no longer seems beautiful. As she left, the doctor was arriving. She raced into the fields and made her way home, down-hearted for Delphine's sake. What would happen to a baby born so early? Would the viscountess be alright? Genevieve recited a prayer as she ran, not stopping till she reached her house.

"Papa, Papa, where are you?" she called as she rushed into the house. Her father emerged from his jewelry studio, wiping his hands.

"Genevieve, what's wrong? You sound so distressed! What happened during your stay at Delphine's? Didn't it go well?"

"No Papa, Delphine and I are fine but her mother is having the baby and it's two months early! What is going to happen to the baby and Delphine's mother?" Genevieve cried.

"Oh, my dear, come here."

He knelt down and took her in his arms. She realized by the sadness in her father's voice that the baby would die. She burst into tears and her heart ached for her new friend's grief. Delphine must have been so excited to have a new brother or sister and now she would have none. Instead, she would have to face death and grief.

Chapter Three

Tragedy had come to the chateau. Sadly, as expected the baby died. Delphine's mother succumbed a few days later. After her mother's death, Delphine was inconsolable, and Genevieve was called upon frequently to come to the chateau to entertain and comfort Delphine. Genevieve was more than happy to help where she could. Often, she simply held Delphine as she cried for her mother. Other times she tried doing funny antics to make Delphine laugh, often imitating comical characters from stories and people from the chateau. This always had the desired effect.

Delphine was especially fond of Genevieve's imitations of Monsieur Joseph, Delphine's private tutor. Monsieur Joseph was an obese man who waddled along holding his protruding abdomen, moaned and groaned as he went up the stairs, then plopped loudly in the small teacher's chair that creaked ominously and barely withstood his weight. He spoke with a high-pitched voice that didn't match with his rotund person. Genevieve knew so much about him because the Viscount Bruneau had included her in Delphine's daily lessons, in an effort to assuage Delphine's sorrow and loneliness since the death of her mother.

Genevieve adored the lessons with Monsieur Joseph. She learned to read quickly and was fascinated by the lessons in geography and history. The thought of traveling to a new country gripped her imagination and she poured over maps and drawings from other lands. Her interest in history lay in examining the motivation of the major players of each country, such as the king and queens, the popes and generals. What led them to make such far reaching decisions? What knowledge or emotions motivated them? Genevieve was like a man dying of thirst who was given a drink. She could not get enough!

Genevieve spent more and more time at the chateau and was even asked to spend the night on occasion if Delphine felt especially lonely. Genevieve was also asked to spend the nights when the Viscount Bruneau was entertaining. He and the servants would all be too busy to attend to Delphine. Often the girls were called down to say goodnight to Delphine's father dressed in their long, thick, linen nightgowns.

On several occasions, Genevieve noticed that a certain gentleman took a distinct interest in them. But instead of being pleased, she felt awkward and uncomfortable. His eyes grazed upon her hair and moved their way down the rest of her. He would then stroke his mustache thoughtfully and smile at her. She invariable blushed and looked away.

He was the only man who sported a mustache as it was not the fashion of the times. A mustache with a beard or goatee was acceptable but a mustache alone was not considered fashionable. Genevieve wondered about this man's need to be different or stand out. He was not unattractive in his way, with his blond hair and blue eyes and strong chin. He wore his hair tied back and sported one earring. His clothes were luxurious, velvets and satins and the whitest cotton shirts beneath his doublet. He even wore a signet ring though Genevieve never got close enough to see the symbol on it. But all in all, there was something animalistic in his appearance and manner that disconcerted Genevieve.

The viscount interrupted Genevieve's thoughts by asking for a goodnight kiss. "Mes Petites, come give me a bissou, a kiss and then off to bed with you!"

As they went to him to give the dutiful kiss, a deep husky voice interrupted them.

"Really viscount, must you make us jealous? Such delightful maidens and you keep all the kisses to yourself."

The viscount laughed and Genevieve could smell the drink on his breath. This coupled with his flushed face and overly jovial manner made Genevieve aware that he was drunk.

"Very well, Robert, have your kisses. Girls, go give your poor lonely uncle Robert a kiss and say goodnight."

"But Papa…" protested Delphine, "He isn't my uncle, and besides I do not know him!"

The viscount face darkened and he responded, "Don't forget your manners, Delphine! Do as you are told."

Genevieve could see the danger in refusing him. Gently she took Delphine's hand and they approached Robert tentatively. He held out his cheek to be kissed first by Delphine and when it came time for Genevieve, he turned his face to her and kissed her on the lips. She was horrified and instinctively wiped her lips with the back of her hand while making a spitting sound, before she could stop herself. He and the viscount would be furious with her poor manners but much to her humiliation, they both burst out laughing.

The viscount said "Robert, she is no fool, is she? She has put you in your place!" and laughed again.

"Yes, quite a little spitfire indeed! But don't think I've learned my lesson. Just wait a few years and things will be different! That I can assure you." he added emphatically.

"Very well, mes petites, off to bed, and sweet dreams."

Delphine and Genevieve raced from the room followed by the sound of laughter and didn't stop till they arrived at Delphine's bedroom and had jumped into bed and snuggled under the covers.

"What a disgraceful and disgusting man that Robert is!" whispered Delphine. "I hope we never see him again but I fear he has become Papa's best friend for now. You were so brave, Genevieve. I wouldn't have dared!"

"I did it without thinking, I was so repulsed and shocked by his lips touching mine!"

She shuddered involuntarily.

"Poor Genny, I'm so sorry you had to be kissed by him!

"What's done is done, but I swear, I will never let myself be kissed by him again!"

Little did Genevieve know what the fates had in mind for her. That night, Genevieve woke in a sweat, recovering from a nightmare. Images of Robert had haunted her dreams all night: his leering face and the taste of wine on his lips. Next time she would be ready, she thought. Next time... and with that comforting thought, she drifted off to sleep.

Chapter four

G enevieve had noticed that after his wife's death, the Viscount had been very despondent and that whenever she was asked to a meal, he drank in abundance and often staggered away from the table. She occasionally came into a chamber to find him weeping or asleep with his mouth agape. If Delphine tried to wake him, he didn't respond.

"My Papa misses my mother so much and the baby he lost was a boy! He loved her so much and now she is gone!" and then Delphine would begin to cry. All Genevieve could do was hold her hand or give her the occasional hug or she might suggest they go play with Spirit to distract her.

As time went by, the viscount did not improve. In fact, every evening he surrounded himself with "friends" who encouraged his drinking and playing of cards. Gambling became his favorite pastime. Genevieve and Delphine did not really understand about gambling but they could tell that he was not in good shape. His constant companion was Monsieur Robert who had all but moved in to the chateau.

The viscount continued to get worse. He spent much of his day in bed; emerging in the evening for a raucous dinner with his entourage and the nightly card game. As the girls woke in the morning, they would come upon Monsieur Robert helping the viscount to his bedchamber after an entire night of gambling. Robert would always stop and make much of the girls.

"My dears, such beautiful girls, such visions. Come and give your Uncle Robert a morning kiss."

The next time Genevieve saw Monsieur Robert was a couple of weeks later. She hadn't given him another thought until she saw him again in the evening as the girls went down to say their good night to Delphine's father. She noticed him immediately when she entered the great hall because he was sitting by the fire alone this time with just the viscount. He seemed somewhat subdued and barely smiled or said good night to the girls. His blue eyes seemed sad when they looked up at the girls and Genevieve felt her heart go out to him.

"Monsieur Robert, you seem so sad tonight. Is anything wrong?" she dared to ask.

"Thank you for your concern, Genevieve. It is sweet of you to notice, Yes, I am sad. My younger sister was ill."

He turned his head to look into the fire.

"Is that why you have been gone?" she asked

"Yes, and in fact she ... died. I had to take care of her burial."

He turned his head away from the girls and stopped speaking.

Genevieve couldn't help herself. She went over and put a hand on his shoulder. Still looking away, he reached up and covered her hand with his and gave it a squeeze.

"I'm so sorry, Monsieur Robert!"

He turned to face her, his blue eyes bright with tears.

"She was so young and full of life. I can't believe she is gone."

He shook his head and gazed back into the fire.

On impulse Genevieve gave him a quick kiss on the cheek before running off to bed.

A week later Monsieur Robert was there again. The viscount had summoned the girls to come say good night. They wrapped shawls around their nightgowns and scurried down to the great hall. As usual several men were drinking with the viscount preparing for their night at cards.

When the girls entered, Monsieur Robert looked up and his handsome face broke into a smile.

"Come girls, Monsieur Robert has something for you, something very special!" said the viscount.

Looking at Monsieur Robert, Genevieve was relieved to see that he was in better spirits than the last time she had seen him. She smiled at him shyly.

When the girls had approached him, he lifted two big boxes onto his lap. Peeking inside, he said, "This one is for you, Delphine, and the other one is for your friend Genevieve. I had them especially made for you!"

Eagerly, the girls approached him. He opened the lid of the top box to reveal something wrapped in soft paper. Carefully, he folded back the paper. There, nestled in the paper, was the most exquisite porcelain doll surrounded by a halo of blond curls, and with beautiful blue eyes. She was dressed in an exquisite blue velvet dress with lace and ribbons all over. Delphine gasped and reached her hands into the box, eagerly pulling the doll to her breast. Then she held it fondly in her arms like a baby.

"Oh, Monsieur Robert, it is exquisite!!!" She gave him a kiss on the cheek. "Now Genevieve's turn," she said and moved aside to make room for her.

Monsieur Robert slowly lifted the lid smiling and when he pulled back the wrappings, Genevieve was amazed to find a doll, that like her, had beautiful red hair and lovely green eyes.

"I had her specially made for you, you see. She looks like you. I had them dye the hair to match your hair and requested green eyes. They were none too pleased with me but they did as they were told. What do you think?"

Genevieve was speechless. She stood with her mouth agape. Slowly, she lifted the doll out of its box and held her lovingly, gazing into her face. Tears came to her eyes, she was so overcome.

"Oh, thank you so much! So much, Monsieur Robert. She looks like me! What shall I call her?!" Genevieve said excitedly.

"Well, perhaps you could call her Lucette, after my sister? But only if you want to," he replied.

"Yes, what a wonderful idea! Lucette is such a pretty name."

She carefully placed the doll on the rug and turning to Robert, gave him a big hug.

"Girls, come sit on my lap with your dolls," begged Robert. Each girl sat on a leg cradling their dolls.

"I'm so glad you are pleased with my gift."

He kissed each girl on the top of her head and the viscount told the girls it was time for bed. Off they went, thanking Monsieur Robert, and clutching their dolls. Back in their bedroom, they kissed their dolls good night, wrapped them in their shawls, and put them together in the doll cradle for the night. They had realized that the dolls were too delicate and fancy to sleep with. Scurrying into bed, Delphine and Genevieve cuddled up for the night, dreaming of Monsieur Robert's gift

After receiving the beautiful dolls from Monsieur Robert, the girls had gotten into the habit of calling him, Uncle Robert and including him in a good night kiss. But this nice interchange did not continue. One evening the girls had stayed up later than usual and when they went to say goodnight, it was obvious that the men had been drinking in full force and already were playing cards. Money and the odd piece of jewelry lay piled in the center of the table.

The viscount was focused on the table and barely responded when the girls went to kiss him good night. Then, as if suddenly remembering something, he turned to Delphine, and slurring his words, said "I may need those earrings I gave you if the cards are bad to me tonight."

Delphine looked shocked that her father was unable to talk clearly and that he was demanding her lovely earrings. But she didn't dare say anything.

"Ah, don't worry, Delphine, your father won't need your earrings. I can always lend him the money if he needs it."

Robert was slurring his words as well though less obviously than the viscount.

"Come here and give me a kiss and then off to bed with you both!" Robert said.

The girls both approached him warily but when they were within close range, he grabbed them and pulled them to him for a kiss. Genevieve dreaded him in this state and rigidly accepted his hug but then he kissed her and gave her a little bite on the neck.

When she tried to pull away, his grip tightened around her waist and he slid his hand down to her bottom and squeezed. Then gave her a spank and pushed her away from him.

"Off you go, lovely ladies! Dream about your Uncle Robert," he said as he turned back to the table.

The girls ran from the room. Delphine, who was very disturbed by her father's words and demeanor, was crying. Genevieve didn't want to add to her distress by telling her what Robert had done. Climbing in bed, she was afraid she would have dreams about him, bad dreams.

The viscount and Robert continued each night drinking and gambling, and the girls no longer enjoyed going for their good night kisses. In fact, they never went unless they were directly summoned. On one such evening, the girls reluctantly approached the viscount and avoided Robert entirely. When he called them over, Delphine, who was afraid to disobey a direct command, approached him and hastily kissed his cheek. But Genevieve was too uncomfortable. She held back and when Robert turned towards her, she simply curtsied, said good night, and grabbing Delphine's hand, fled from the room.

The next morning, the girls found Robert stumbling down the hall after a heavy night of drinking. He had already deposited the viscount in his bed and was heading down the hall to the bed chamber where he often stayed. Seeing the girls, he stopped, and leaning against the wall, he called them to him. Delphine obeyed and received a sloppy morning kiss dutifully on the forehead. Genevieve knew what would be in store for her with Robert in this shape.

"Good morning, Monsieur Robert" she said dropping a curtsy.

"What! MONSIEUR Robert is it? Not Uncle Robert?" he replied in a surly tone.

He lunged toward her and grabbing her arm, put his face close to hers saying, "Miss High and Mighty, are you? Too good for the likes of me? One day you'll be sorry you snubbed your Uncle Robert. Just you wait!"

Releasing her, he lurched back against the wall to steady himself and spit on the floor in front of her. Indignant and afraid, the girls ran back down the hall to their room, locking the door behind them.

"What has happened to Uncle Robert? Why is he so angry and unpleasant now?" Delphine asked, visibly shaken. "Why does he hate us?"

"It's not you he hates, you are still the obedient little girl. It is me he is angry at because I am reluctant to treat him like I did before. Now he is drinking so much, he seems like a totally different person! I can't believe we ever considered him as an uncle, can you?" Genevieve responded.

"And Papa, is he drinking too much as well? Is that what is wrong with him, why he needs help getting to bed and sleeps all day?"

"Oh Delphine, I thought you knew but now I see how could you know, you have never had to witness men who are drunk before now. Yes, that is what is wrong with your Papa. I'm so sorry!"

"And does Uncle Robert do nothing to stop Papa?"

"Sadly, no. I think he encourages him to drink with him. It is their way to forget their sorrows. Our neighbor in the village drank and there were plenty of nights where my father had to go to his house to protect his wife and children from his drunken rage."

"But what happened to them?"

"One winter night, he went raging into the night and never returned. A few days later, they found him frozen to death. It was horrible."

"But what can we do to help my father?"

"There is nothing we can do until he is ready and as long as Monsieur Robert is here, he'll not change his ways. All we can do is pray."

Chapter Five

The summer was unlike any other that Genevieve had ever experienced. The heat hung like a cloak on everything and the humidity infected every inch of space. Mold began to grow on the walls of the house and sweat poured down every inch of Genevieve's body. The laborers were dropping like flies in the heat and were having to be carried to their homes to recuperate.

Her father had had to stop his metal work because the heat in the forge was unbearable. He worked on his more delicate pieces, his jewelry commissions but that work did not last long. Genevieve spent much of her time in the relative cool of the forest or cooling off in the local stream, beginning by only dipping her feet in the cool waters. As she saw how much the other children enjoyed dunking themselves in the stream, she slowly began to put more and more of herself in the water. It was so refreshing. The children splashed each other, giggling in delight.

Often, she was invited to the chateau to visit with Delphine. That was always a god-send because the chateau was dark and remarkably cool. They would play in Delphine's room rather than play outside on the chateau grounds.

And then the dreaded sickness came to Genevieve's village: Cholera. That's what the doctor called it and told Genevieve's father to send her to stay at the isolated safety of the chateau if the viscount would allow it. Her father immediately gave her a message to take to the chateau, and on the chance that the answer was Yes, he packed her clothes and quickly sent her on her way. He stood watching at the door as she walked to the forest to make her way to Delphine's home. Glancing back, Genevieve saw the distress on her father's face. She paused and yelled back at him:

"I love you, Papa! I will see you soon!"

He waved and blew her a kiss, yelling back that she was more precious to him than his life.

That was the last thing he ever said to her. The cholera swept through the village and by the end of the month, half the villagers were dead, including her father.

Genevieve received the news through Pere LeMaitre. He had given her father his last rites. The dead were buried in a communal grave because of the large accumulation of bodies. Pere LeMaitre and the doctor were both miraculously spared from the cholera and were given the unpleasant task of overseeing the burials.

Genevieve would always remember the moment she heard of her beloved father's death. It was late afternoon and a blessed rain had begun to fall, not just a light rain but a down pour. Delphine and Genevieve rejoiced at the break in the heat and had run outside to dance in the rain. They were soon drenched and joyfully continued to dance and sing in the rain. The viscount had come to the door to usher them in but seeing their joy, he simply stood watching them.

That was when they noticed Pere LeMaitre on his horse. He had obviously been caught in the rain. He reined in his horse, descended as quickly as his old frame would allow, and rushed up the steps to take shelter in the entrance of the chateau. The viscount welcomed him in and they disappeared into the chateau.

Their curiosity piqued, the girls decided to follow in their wake to see why Pere LeMaitre had come. Dripping, they stood in the main hall to listen to him. He turned to them with a pained look on his face, and the viscount was frowning. What were they talking about? Genevieve wondered.

"Papa, what is wrong? You look so distressed?" Delphine cried and rushed to him to comfort him, throwing her arms around him. Slowly he pulled her arms from around him and approached Genevieve. He knelt in front of her and took both her hands as Pere LeMaitre came and stood behind her with his hand on her shoulder.

"Genevieve, I have some bad news. Your father caught the sickness a week ago. He fought valiantly but God saw fit to take him. He received his last rites so he will be with God in heaven and is sure to be looking down on you."

Genevieve began trembling uncontrollably. The words were echoing, ringing in her head. Screaming "No!", and before anyone could stop her, she raced out of the hall and out of the chateau.

"They must be wrong! They have made a mistake!" She repeated over and over as she raced through the rain, through the fields, the forest to the village.

When she finally arrived, shaking, she opened the door to her home calling out to her father. The stillness made her frantic. She raced to his workshop crying "Papa, are you there? It's me, Genevieve. I need you!"

But no one was there. The silence was deafening. Genevieve felt a sharp pain in her heart and collapsed on the floor wailing, "Papa, Papa, how could you leave me?" over and over.

After what seemed a long while, her sobbing stopped. She gathered herself up from the floor and slowly and reverently walked amongst the things that most made her think of her father. And then she saw it, a slip of paper on the table with an object on it. She rushed to the table and saw her father's writing. It read; "For you, my beloved daughter, remember I love you always. Papa."

Lying on the piece of paper was a necklace of silver with a miniature unicorn hanging from it. A beautiful, exquisite unicorn made by her father for her. He must have remembered how taken she was with the story of "The Lady and the Unicorn". Weeping, she kissed the note and rested it against her cheek muttering "Papa, Papa". Folding the note with great care, she tucked it into her gown, placing it against her heart. She took the necklace and gazed at the lovely unicorn. Gently she placed it around her neck.

What must she do now? She had no father, no mother. She sat wondering what to do when she heard a horse approaching. A rap came at the door and it was flung open. There was the viscount.

He pulled her to her feet and taking her outside, he put her on his horse, while she protested. "My father, my father! He's gone! He's gone!"

The viscount leapt onto his horse and off they flew, as quickly as possible, away from the village of death.

Chapter Six

After the death of her father, Genevieve moved into the Chateau. Delphine, though very sorry for Genevieve's sorrow, was thrilled to have her living there like a real and true sister. The viscount welcomed her without a second thought. He knew how much she meant to his daughter and he was a kind hearted man in his own right. Genevieve was given her own bedchamber but more nights than not, she slept in Delphine's bed, seeking comfort from the presence of her dear friend.

The weeks past and Genevieve began to feel glimmers of life return to her spirit. Her eleventh birthday came and Delphine and the viscount had planned a special gift.

"Come with us!" Delphine said pulling Genevieve in her excitement. They led her to the door of the chateau. Jumping up and down, Delphine exclaimed "Are you ready?"

Puzzled, Genevieve nodded. The viscount slowly opened the door. There stood the groom Henri holding the reins of the horse she had named Chestnut.

"What is Chestnut doing here? Are we going somewhere?" asked Genevieve in confusion.

"What is Chestnut doing here? That is your gift. Chestnut. He is to be your horse and Henri is going to teach you how to ride! Isn't that perfect?" Delphine answered, clapping in delight.

"I hope you are pleased, Genevieve. It was all Delphine's idea. She knows how often you go to visit Chestnut in his stall and help brush him and care for him. I asked Henri if he thought you were too young to learn to ride but he said it would be fine, as long as you are firm with the horse," the viscount chimed in.

"Pleased? Pleased? I am overjoyed! '" she exclaimed and ran to give the viscount a hug, then grabbed Delphine's hand and raced down the steps where Chestnut was pacing restlessly in place. Genevieve threw her arms around Chestnut's neck and buried her nose in the familiar scent of his neck.

"Chestnut, Chestnut, you are mine now. Mine! We can learn to ride the grounds together!"

She looked up into his deep brown eyes and recognized again the kindred spirit in him. She had not dared give her heart fully to him before because she knew he was the viscount's horse and made to draw the carriage. It bothered her to see him labor under the weight of the carriage but now, now she could protect and love him completely and unabashedly.

"When can I start my lessons?!" she asked Henri. Henri was a young man of eighteen, the stable boy well versed in the knowledge of horses and riding. He was often sent on errands into the village on horseback. Genevieve knew he would be a good teacher. Henri looked up at the viscount for a sign of his approval.

"Well, how about a walk? Delphine can go with you, if that's alright."

The girls eagerly were helped upon Chestnut's back but the second he started walking, Delphine cried out in fear. Henri stopped the horse immediately and Delphine begged to be let down again. Genevieve was secretly pleased to have Chestnut all to herself and leaned down to pat his neck. Their walk continued slowly for a time while the viscount and Delphine watched. Finally, the viscount shouted he was going inside and disappeared into the chateau. Delphine sat herself down on the steps to continue watching. To

Genevieve it was like a communion of souls. She felt so strongly the bond between them even going at such a slow pace. She moved as he moved, as one, fluid and strong.

Genevieve was a quick learner, which was helped by the strong trust she felt for her horse. Henri was always happy to see her during the lessons and pleased with her progress. He was a kind boy and not bad looking. His family lived in the village and Genevieve had known his younger sisters when she had lived there. She often thought of the difference in their circumstances and how that one fateful day, when she had found Spirit, had changed her life and her prospects so entirely. It made her wonder about God's plan. It didn't make sense to her that some should have and others have not, some should suffer and others... Well, suffering was universal, death came to all regardless of one's circumstances. It was the great equalizer.

Genevieve stopped her musings and asked after his sisters. "Henri, how are Marie and Catherine?"

"Marie, like your father, was lost in the summer of the Cholera, but Catherine is married now and expecting her first child." he replied.

"Married?! But she was only a couple of years older than me!"

"Yes, she knew she was with child and needed to marry. That is the way in the village. It is natural for a young girl to start to bear children as soon as possible. Life is short, especially in the village."

Genevieve thought about herself. She was still such a child at eleven. She couldn't imagine being married in a few years, and having children on top of that. Thoughtfully, she brushed Chestnut and was grateful yet again for the good circumstances she lived in.

Genevieve soon became an expert rider. She would fly over the roads and fields on Chestnut, riding in the bliss of two moving as one. But her joy in riding led to her frequent visits to the stables. It was on one of these occasions that Robert appeared just when Henri was helping her up onto her horse. Genevieve was in such a joyous mood. It was a crisp fall day and she felt exhilarated. Her face was beaming. Robert immediately flew into a rage at the sight.

"What are you doing, young man?! How dare you touch a mistress of the house! How dare you, with your filthy hands and dirty mind!"

He flew at him with his crop, whipping Henri as he cowered in the corner of the stall.

"Stop, stop! It's not his fault. I asked him. Stop it now!" Genevieve cried in horror.

Robert turned his anger on her and gave her horse a harsh whip with the crop. Chestnut, unused to such treatment, reared in the stall and Genevieve fell off his back, hitting her head in the fall. Chestnut raced off neighing angrily and Genevieve lay in the straw of his stall, unconscious.

Henri immediately bent to help her but Robert pushed him roughly aside and picked Genevieve up in his arms, cursing his own stupidity. He carried her to the chateau amazed at the lightness of her little frame. It struck him that she was just a child but he shook the thought from his mind.

Genevieve was placed in her bed, attended to by Collette, the old nurse maid from Delphine's younger days. She mopped Genevieve's brow and shook her gently to see if she would awaken. The doctor was sent for and administered a draught and said all they could do was wait. So wait they did in a great state of agitation.

Robert had not confessed his part in her accident. He blamed Henri instead and suggested that the boy be dismissed. Despite his protests, Henri was indeed dismissed for his imagined part in the fiasco. No one bothered to listen to his story as he was just a stable boy. That he dared to refute Robert's story was reason enough to dismiss him.

"I never liked that young man, the way he looked at Genevieve! It wasn't right. It was downright disgusting. He deserved to be whipped! Dismissing him was letting him off easy!" Robert stated to the viscount.

It was three days later that Genevieve awoke, groggy and aching. She had no memory of what had happened and was shocked to hear that Chestnut had misbehaved. Something must have set him off but with Henri gone, she would never know. Still her trust in her horse was strong enough to survive this mishap.

There was such joy in the chateau because of her recovery that a celebration was called for. While Delphine sat by Genevieve's bedside, the viscount and his friends caroused in the great hall, drinking to excess as was their way.

Chapter Seven

A year passed and one day Delphine and Genevieve were playing in the garden. Delphine was surrounded by all her dolls and they were having a tea party. A sudden chill filled the air and she shivered. Genevieve knew that Delphine was not a hearty child and was prone to illness.

"Delphine, would you like your shawl? I can fetch it quickly for you."

"Oh, would you mind? I'm all settled here with the dolls and I am not as fast as you are, especially with all those stairs."

Genevieve ran off to Delphine's room and as she came down the corridor, someone came out of the viscount's chamber into the dark hall. Much to her dismay, she realized too late that it was Monsieur Robert. She stopped in her tracks and he quickly approached her.

"Well, if it isn't my favorite little lady! What a pleasant surprise!" he said grabbing her hand. She squirmed nervously.

"I must be a lucky man to have this opportunity to see you alone. There is something I have been meaning to ask you. You are of age now to be thinking about marriage. I fancy you as my wife. How does that sound to you? I'll soon be a very rich man and you could hardly do better, a penniless girl like you. I'll speak to the viscount about it."

Genevieve was speechless. Marriage? She knew that twelve years of age was barely an acceptable age for marriage and she hadn't gone through any changes in her body yet and still considered herself a child. Why was this man suggesting this?

"I…I…am just a child of twelve. I'm not ready!" she exclaimed.

"Ready? You are a beauty. You must realize that. You will become a woman soon and I will teach you how to be a good and willing wife."

Reaching up with his free hand, he ran his fingers through her long auburn tresses.

"No! No! Stop it!" she yelled trying to pull away.

Suddenly his grip on her hair tightened and she was caught. He pushed her against the wall, pressing his body against hers and pulling her head back. Before she knew what was happening, he had his mouth on hers and she felt his tongue entering her mouth. Every inch of her was repulsed and she gagged and kicked. She began to scream once her mouth was free but he pushed his hand over her mouth to stop her. Before she knew it, she bit his hand. He yelped in pain and in his surprise, leapt away from her.

Seeing her chance, she rushed down the corridor as fast as she could and raced outside. Should she tell Delphine what had happened? Delphine seemed blissfully ignorant of Genevieve's state and was playing happily with her dolls. Better to keep her that way. She handed Delphine her shawl and settled down on the grass with her back to the rose bushes. She did not want anyone sneaking up on her, especially Monsieur Robert!

Soon after the unpleasant episode, Genevieve found Delphine crying miserably in her room. When Delphine saw Genevieve, she threw herself into her arms and sobbed loudly.

"Delphine! What is wrong?! Tell me! I'm so worried, is your father alright?"

All Genevieve could imagine was that the viscount was dead. What else could cause so much unhappiness?

Delphine pulled away and wiped her tear-stained face.

"No Papa is fine, if you can call it that, what with the way he drinks, but he has done something disastrous. He has gambled away our entire fortune, and… and… he has lost the chateau to Monsieur Robert! But that's not the worst part. He wants me to marry Robert! He says we will be driven penniless from the chateau but if I can get Monsieur Robert to marry me, I, at least, will have a home. But how can I?" she wailed and bursting back into tears, threw herself upon her bed.

"What! Marry Monsieur Robert! But how could you bear it? How could your father expect such a thing?!"

Genevieve felt sickened by the news and she didn't know which news was worst: that they were homeless or that frail, delicate Delphine would be married to Monsieur Robert? She was still such a child and so fragile. She could not imagine Delphine surviving such a marriage. In her anger, Genevieve rushed from the room to confront the viscount and with the hope that Delphine was misinformed.

When she reached the main hall, she was out of breath. The viscount was slouched in his chair with his head in his hands, while Robert stood above him, his back to her.

"You know, I will quite like being lord of the chateau and the title of viscount added to my name. You are a nothing now."

The viscount muttered "I've been a fool, a drunken fool and now my daughter will have to pay for my debts. If you marry Delphine, I would be somewhat at peace knowing she is safe and taken care of."

"So, it's true? Everything Delphine told me is true? You have lost everything and Delphine must marry? How could you do this to her?" sputtered Genevieve.

Robert turned at the sound of her voice and his obvious pleasure enraged her. Before she could stop herself, she threw herself at him, beating him with her small fists.

"You monster! You planned it all! You're a pig, a viper! I hate you!"

Robert had grabbed her wrists and in a tone of half anger and half amusement said: "Ah, my favorite red head, you little vixen. It is really you I would have for my wife.

Why would I want his plain, feeble daughter? She would most likely die giving me an heir. You are a much better specimen in all ways: looks, strength and spirit! Taming you will be a thrill. Maybe we can come to some arrangement."

"Arrangement? I would never marry you, not after you tricked Delphine's father like that, pretending to be his friend so you could steal from him."

"Steal? I won it fair and square. Who are you to speak to me in this way, you, a snippet of a girl without a penny to your name! But I have a proposition for you. You wouldn't like to see the viscount and Delphine living on the streets, and you too. They have been good to you, very good. The viscount has treated you like a daughter with all the advantages and education you could want. You will grow into an elegant, educated young lady and coupled with your beauty, you would make me proud to have you as my wife. You are strong and healthy and will be sure to bear me sons.

So here is my proposition. You can save the viscount and your dear Delphine from poverty and a life on the streets by marrying me. They could go live in my old house and I would support them, modestly of course. But they would be comfortable and cared for. You might even have her come to visit, on occasion."

At Robert's words, the viscount looked up with a glimmer of hope in his eyes.

"What, would you do that, Robert? Genevieve, please, you can save us all from ruin and disaster. Please, please, Genevieve, think of everything we have done for you?" the viscount said, slipping to his knees and wringing his hands in front of her.

Genevieve's mind was spinning. What was he saying, that the fate of her beloved Delphine, literally her life was in her hands? Delphine would never survive on the streets and the viscount had been good to her over the years, raising her like a daughter, taking her in when her father died. They were all she had in this world. And where would she go? The full weight of the situation hit her. She thought she would faint and staggered back into a chair.

"Please Genevieve, our fate is in your hands, you can save us!" exclaimed the viscount with outstretched arms and tears flowing.

What could she do? She had no one but them and she could save them and herself. What was marriage anyway? A fairy tale? Or something to be treasured? She wasn't one given to dreams of romance. Would it be so terrible to be married to Robert? She shuddered at the thought. But she would be mistress of the chateau and Delphine could still visit. Was she a coward or was she brave enough to face this? How could she possibly say no in the face of what would happen to them.

She held her sickened stomach and, barely above a whisper, said, "Very well, I will be your wife."

She ran from the room as quickly as she could and rushed outside into the fields, running until she reached the dark silence of the forest.

"My God, what have I done?!" She lay down on a soft bed of pine needles and cried herself to sleep.

When Genevieve woke, it was dark out and the moon was shining through the trees. She momentarily forgot where she was and slowly felt the ground under her hands. The smell of pine needles filled the air. She sat herself up, brushing the needles from her dress. With great reluctance, she rose to her feet. Slowly she made her way out of the forest and entered the open space of the wheat fields that surrounded the chateau. Moon light flooded the night sky and gave the wheat a blue hue. The moon cast shadows on the towers of the chateau and reflected off the stones in a brilliant white. The beauty of the scene took her breath away but then her melancholy returned full force.

She entered quietly and made her way to her bed chamber. There, lying asleep, was Delphine clutching her favorite doll. Genevieve looked fondly on the blond-haired girl who was like a sister to her. How young and defenseless she looked! Genevieve kissed her finger and gently placed it on Delphine's soft cheek. Delphine stirred and opened her eyes.

"Genevieve, Genevieve, I've been waiting for you. My father told me you are going to save us by marrying Monsieur Robert. I can't tell you how much I love you for this. I know I am a weakling, a coward, But I don't think I could have survived such a life. Do you forgive me?"

"Yes, of course I forgive you. You are more important to me than anyone or anything in the world. What would I have done without your friendship and your father's? It's time for me to grow up and repay my debt to both of you."

"But Monsieur Robert! I'm so sorry for you. He has always had a particular interest in you but I never thought it was that kind of interest. How will you survive?"

"Delphine, I will survive and we must never talk of this again. I have made up my mind and I must go through with this for all our sakes. So let's go to sleep and greet tomorrow with a brave face."

"Very well, Genevieve, good night," and she shyly added, "I love you."

"I love you too," Genevieve said wearily and removing her dress, she climbed into bed for a restless night's sleep.

Chapter Eight

The magnitude of Genevieve's despair grew as her wedding day approached. One night in her agitation, she knew that sleep would not come to her. Instead, she paced the room, back and forth, wondering how she would survive this loveless marriage especially to a man like Robert. His behavior repulsed and even frightened her and tomorrow she would be his.

Genevieve paused in her pacing and stood in front of the window. She pressed her forehead against the cold glass and gazed at the ground below. Gently she tapped her head against the glass, deep in thought. Her room was three stories from the ground. It was a long way down. Slowly she opened the window and leaned out. Yes, it was a long way down. Certainly, she would not survive if she fell. If she were dead, she would not have to marry and become Robert's victim, his slave, for the rest of her life. She would not have to lie in bed waiting for his version of passion, or have to bear his children. She would be free of the miseries of her existence, and be blessedly reunited with her parents.

As Genevieve's mind raced with these thoughts, she leaned further out the window, imaging the fall, the air enveloping her, her limbs flung out, free as a bird. Finally, the fear of the impact. Of course, Delphine would be heart broken. and what was to stop Robert from carrying out his plan to evict the viscount and Delphine. Her death would solve nothing.

With tears streaming down her face, Genevieve took one final look at the ground beneath her and slowly closed the window. In final defeat, she threw herself upon her bed and sobbed.

There was nothing to be done. She would have to marry Robert.

Robert wanted the marriage to take place without delay. Did he think Genevieve would change her mind once the shock of her decision wore off? He wanted it to be a grand occasion, when he could show off his glorious prize to the world. He bought her the most sumptuous gown of velvets and satins that he could find, and to advertise her virginity, it was all in shades of white. How anyone could doubt the virginity of someone so young, Genevieve had no idea. The gown was tight and pushed up her small breasts, making them seem larger as they pressed out of the top of her gown. She blushed when she saw this but there was little she could do to make herself look more modest.

Robert had ridden ahead to arrive at the church first. She would come in the carriage with Delphine and the viscount. He would play the part of her father, to lead her down the aisle and give her away. It was a somber group that climbed into the carriage to go to church. Delphine would precede Genevieve down the aisle to be prepared to take her bouquet when the time came. As a result, Robert had also bought her a beautiful gown but she was hardly able to enjoy it under the circumstances. Robert had paid for a priest from Paris to come for the ceremony. Pere LeMaitre was too simple a man for his tastes. The church was packed with Robert's friends, a variety of people and somewhat suspect.

Genevieve descended from the carriage and faltered at the entrance of the church. What was she doing? The enormity of her decision and its dreaded consequences hit her and she stopped. Delphine gently took her hand and led her into the shadowed darkness of the church. The viscount took her arm in his and patted her hand in comfort. When the music started, Genevieve made her way down the aisle, the beauty of the music completely escaping her. All she heard was a roaring in her ears and all she felt was a tightening of her stomach and a wave of nausea. She felt she was going to her death, a spiritual death and that her life would be forever sealed.

At the altar, Robert stood firm and proud. He did not turn to look at her, rather he stood with his hands behind his back facing the priest. Genevieve's bouquet shook as she trembled upon reaching his side. Delphine took it from her, glancing lovingly and encouragingly at her. Genevieve went through the motions of the ceremony detached from herself. She felt she was floating above her body watching someone else. Robert was a tall man and she felt she must look tiny beside him. She certainly felt tiny inside. The only blessing of the entire event was the knowledge that she would not have to perform her 'wifely duties' that night or for many to come.

Robert had hired a midwife to examine her before the marriage. He wanted to be sure she could provide him with an heir. Genevieve's examination was painful with all its poking and prodding. The midwife, Therese, was a kind woman but regardless, it was intrusive and, Genevieve felt, it was unnecessary and humiliating. She secretly hoped she would be found unsuitable but then thought better of it. She had to go through with this to help herself, Delphine and the viscount.

The midwife washed her hands and gently raised Genevieve back to a sitting position, pulling her chemise down over her.

Genevieve held her breath as Robert was ushered into the room. The good news to Genevieve was that though she was capable of bearing children, she was not physically ready for it. She had not had her first woman's blood so no child could be conceived. As well, she was not fully grown and her hips were still too close together to deliver a baby. The midwife had told her after an examination that even if her first blood came, she was not equipped to be Robert's wife or lover. She was much too tiny to receive him and her hips were still too delicate and close, still growing, to carry a baby to term. At best, she might carry a stillborn child to four months and lose it with great pain with great risk to herself.

The midwife Therese had commiserated with Genevieve while Robert waited in the next room.

"Of course, love, it's his decision. After all you're just a female and dispensable as far as he is concerned and most of the world is concerned! If you died tomorrow, what would he care? All he needs is a breeding machine. That's what purpose we women serve, baby breeders, that's all. Perhaps you too were raised to believe your wifely duties are more important than your life, like most of us, yes, very likely since you were married off at such a sinfully inappropriate age!"

She had gone on with bitterness, under her breath, muttering, "Who did this to this child, what bloody madman would send his daughter to a fate like this?"

She had furiously packed away her herbs, salves and implements in her basket, preparing to leave the place she found so distasteful.

Robert took the news gracefully enough, nodding and glancing at Genevieve as she got dressed in the corner. He showed some disappointment but being who he was, Genevieve had expected anger. Genevieve gave a huge sigh of relief when he left the room. Suddenly she felt a hand on her shoulder. Turning around, she was confronted with the midwife's kind face.

"My dear, you are too young for this marriage. Must you go through with it? The doctor has told me that Monsieur Robert is a very big man, in his manly parts. Any intercourse could do serious damage to you and perhaps prevent you from delivering children in the future. You must absolutely be sure to hold off on your wifely duties until you have grown some more and until I tell you. Do you understand? I will speak to your husband at greater length about this after I have left you."

Madame Therese made her promise, gave her a brief embrace and went on her way, leaving Genevieve so much happier than she had expected to be. Now if she could make sure Robert kept his word. She suspected he would wait. He wouldn't want to take any chance of spoiling her ability to give him his precious heir.

After the ceremony was over, Robert led her down the aisle, out of the church and into the sunlight. Back at the chateau, she sat by his side at the great table that was laden with all sorts of tempting fare. But Genevieve absently picked at her food and put on a smile every time someone came up to speak to her. Robert drank and laughed and glowed in the sheer pleasure of having made her his wife. Genevieve could not imagine how he could be happy to have a child wife who didn't even love him. How could he be so happy? The ways of love escaped her.

That evening after everyone had gone for the night, she told Robert she was exhausted and was ready to go to sleep. She rose from the table and started to leave the hall.

"Where do you think you are going, Genevieve? You are my wife. You go when and where I tell you, and you will come to me and kiss me good night!" Robert protested. "And then we will go to our bedchamber together!"

Our bedchamber? The words rang in her head. Was he not going to keep his word?

"But...I thought I would be sleeping in my own chamber." she stammered.

"Your chamber? You are my wife now and I want you by my side. You will come with me now."

He took her arm and whistled a happy tune as they made their way to his bed chamber.

With great reluctance she allowed him to steer her into the room. He began to undress and threw his doublet on a chair. He sat himself on the bed and continued to undress. She stood on the other side of the bed where he could not see her and slowly disrobed until she was in her full-length chemise. Robert was soon naked but for his long shirt which to Genevieve's great relief, covered his manly parts. He climbed in bed looking at her and lifted the covers on her side of the bed.

"Come on, I'm not going to bite you!"

Genevieve stood uncertainly until Robert reached out and took her hand.

"Come, my dear. I know I must not ask you to perform your wifely duties, so you are safe. I am tired and want to go to sleep now so please hurry."

Genevieve knew waiting would stop nothing, perhaps might even change his good mood to anger. Carefully she climbed under the covers and lay rigidly with her back to him.

"What, no good night kiss?" He paused hoping for some response. "Very well," he said in disappointment as he rolled over, blew out the candle and was soon asleep. Genevieve slept fitfully throughout the night, hardly daring to move from her rigid position from the edge of the bed. Robert slept peacefully, breathing evenly. Genevieve must have fallen asleep because, in the early dawn, she found herself wrapped in Robert's arms. She held her breath in horror and hardly dared to move. But move she must to get out of this distasteful situation. Slowly she lifted his arm from around her and inched away from his body. He was awakened by the movement and grabbing her gently, pulled her back to his side.

"Where are you off to so early? Come and snuggle with your new husband." A tone of joy was in his voice.

What could she say? He pulled her to him and kissed her on the forehead. She wriggled around to put her back to him. Slowly, ever so slowly, her muscles relaxed inch by inch. She allowed him to whisper in her ear about his hopes and dreams until the sun rose fully and the serving maid knocked on the door with their morning meal.

"Nourishment, ma maître?"

"Come in," he called releasing Genevieve and sitting up. She scrambled to sit up and cover herself with her knees pulled up to her chest.

Would everyone wonder if she had given Robert her virginity? Would everyone be talking? She felt deeply embarrassed as the serving maid smirked when she presented the tray to Robert.

"I trust you slept well?" she asked as she curtsied and back out of the room.

They ate their meal in silence and then Robert hopped out of bed, splashed water on his face and dressed. As he turned to leave, he said "Good day, my wife! I will see you later," and was gone.

Grateful at his departure, Genevieve quickly dressed and made her way to her own bedroom. She undressed and climbed into her own cozy bed and was soon asleep.

PART TWO:
Marriage

Chapter One

As one lazy day after another wore on, Robert began to get restless. Genevieve noticed his lack of patience with the servants and pretty soon it spread to her.

"What kind of wife are you? Just in name? What have I gotten myself into!" he would tell her at dinner and then drink to excess. Genevieve rarely slept in his bed after the first night and his drinking had become such that he had to be helped to his bed chamber by a servant. He did not seem to notice her absence and slept late into the day. Genevieve was relieved by his new schedule and spent her mornings riding Chestnut, doing embroidery, and weaving on the new tapestry loom that Robert had gotten her. Her dream was to make a unicorn tapestry. For her, the unicorn would always remind her of her bond with her father. She still wore the necklace every day except when Robert required her to decorate herself in jewels if guests were coming to dinner. The jewels were heavy and cumbersome and she felt like a fool at her age sporting such finery.

Robert's drinking became worse and his mood became surly. Now he would ride off in the evening and not reappearing till morning, throw himself in bed till the late afternoon. Genevieve had no illusions about where Robert went during the nights. He must have been with other women and though the thought repulsed her, she was grateful that he wasn't with her.

The distance between them grew and grew. He cursed her and barely looked at her. She stayed out of his way as much as possible.

As the months went on Genevieve noticed that her body was changing. She now had real breasts, small though they were. Her hips were wider and she had a waist. She prayed that Robert would not notice the changes and wore her clothes loosely to hide her figure.

"You are getting fat!" he snarled at her one evening before he set off. "I don't want a pig for a wife! I will tell the cook, no more sweet foods for you," he finished as he strode out of the room.

And then the unthinkable happened. Robert left in the early evening and when he returned a couple of hours later, he was not alone. Genevieve heard him staggering down the corridor and peeking out saw he was moving along with the help of a woman.

"Well, aren't I the lucky girl. Of all the ladies, you chose me to come back with you! They will all be jealous."

She giggled as Robert squeezed her tightly to him and when he kissed her long and hard, she moaned in pleasure.

Horrified, Genevieve shut her door and rested against it, feeling shocked and mortified. What was he thinking to bring his women to their home? How was she to bear it? His drinking and lust seemed insatiable.

The night came when Robert arrived home with two women. If Genevieve thought it couldn't get any worse, she was seriously wrong. For that night, her door swung open and Robert came to her bed, grabbed her arm and pulled her out of bed.

"Robert, what are you doing?! Please leave me alone! You are obviously busy. You don't need me."

"You are my wife and you need to learn the ways of love-making so you can be prepared for when the time comes! You are coming with me right now!"

There was little she could do in the face of his strength. She struggled and kicked but he dragged her down the hall to his room.

He pushed her into the room and turned and locked the door. The two women were already in his bed and were vaguely surprised to see Genevieve.

"What, two is not enough for you?!" one of them said laughing. "Or do you prefer them extra young? Are we too mature for you?"

"This is my wife and she needs to learn a few things about the world of pleasuring a man. She will watch and take note."

He grabbed a chair from against the wall and pulled it near the bed. "Now sit down and be quiet and do what I say, understand?!" Robert growled at Genevieve.

He shoved her in the chair and she immediately struggled to her feet. He shoved her again but she continued to struggle.

"Damn you! If you don't sit still, I'm going to tie you up!" Hearing this, she stopped her struggle.

Robert threw off his clothes and Genevieve immediately closed her eyes. She had managed to never see him naked and it was a shock to her. She sensed that Robert had climbed into the bed. When Genevieve's closed eyes began to ache, they fluttered open momentarily. She quickly shut her eyes again but the imagine she had seen was burned into her brain and made her sick to her stomach. She gritted her teeth in frustration and ran from the chair, banging on the door, hoping a servant might hear her. No luck.

It seems an eternity before Robert collapsed on the bed. She was so upset, she knew she would never forgive him, never! Robert quickly fell asleep and one of the women climbed softly out of bed and unlocked the door. Genevieve thanked her and ran trembling to her room. Tears of rage filled her eyes. She climbed into bed and shook herself all over to rid herself of the filth of Robert's actions. But she couldn't sleep, instead curling herself up into a little ball and weeping.

The following day was Sunday and Genevieve and Robert always attended services. Confession was the only time see was allowed out of Robert's sight. Pere LeMaitre listened patiently to her youthful confessions.

In a whisper, Genevieve said, " Forgive me father, for I have sinned. I have sinned against my husband because I have wished him dead. I have prayed for it! I have asked forgiveness of our Lord. Please forgive me in his stead."

"My child, to pray for someone's death is truly a sin. But why do you pray for this?"

"Last night he made me watch…watch him with other women!"

"Watch him with other women? What do you mean?"

"In bed, Mon Père, doing things!" she whispered mortified. There was a long silence. "How old are you, my child?"

"Twelve years old, Mon Pere."

"I see, you are too young for this sort of life. My child, you are forgiven for your sins but remember to come to confession every Sunday and tell me how you are doing. Now say ten Hail Mary's for the good of your soul."

Genevieve had come to dread each evening, wondering if a repeat performance would occur. And then the thing she had been worrying about since her marriage vows happened. One morning she woke to find blood on her sheet. She immediately understood what it meant, and yanking the sheet off of her bed, she carried it to the fire place, stoked up the embers into a flame and tossed in the sheet.

In a complete panic, she dressed quickly and hurried to the stables. The groom was half asleep but she roused him and told him she must have Chestnut ready immediately. As soon as the horse was saddled, she jumped on his back and rode to the village at a gallop. She knew where the midwife lived and she knew she had to speak to her.

People were awake in the village and curious eyes looked at her. Humiliated, she stared straight ahead and ignored them. She had no way to explain herself. At the midwife's cottage, she rapped on the door after tying Chestnut to a tree.

"Madame Therese, are you there?" she called out in her impatience."

The door swung open and the midwife, visibly surprised ushered her in.

"Goodness me, what is the matter? Are you alright?" Therese inquired as she led Genevieve to a chair by the fire.

"Oh Madame Therese, it's happened. I woke this morning to find blood on my sheet! Do you know what this means?! It means I will have to perform my wifely duties now and I am so terrified of my husband and I'm so fearful that it will hurt and I will die in childbirth because my body is not ready! What can I do?!" she cried.

"My dear girl, it's not as bad as all that. First let me help you with your monthly bleeding."

After that was taken care of, Madame Therese talked about her wifely duties.

"The first time will hurt, it is true but after that, if you use oils and salves that I will give you, you should adjust but be sure your husband gives you time to use them or you could do damage to yourself. And remember, my dear, you are not alone, all women go through this."

Giving Genevieve a quick hug, she handed her two jars, tightly sealed which Genevieve placed carefully in her satchel.

"Thank you so much, Madame Therese!" and feeling slightly comforted, she headed back to the chateau.

Chapter Two

G enevieve thought she might hide her condition from her husband for as long as possible. She wrote to Delphine to come and help her, or at least give her some solace. She had not seen her since her wedding over a year ago and though she wrote to her often and asked Robert if Delphine could come, he always said no. Feeling all alone and desperate, she had decided not to ask for his permission. Her despair must have come through in her letter because, to Genevieve's delight, Delphine wrote back that she would come.

Genevieve knew it was a long trip and she worried about Delphine. But she put her worries aside. Two days later, a carriage came up the drive of the chateau and Genevieve raced outside to greet her friend. There were great tears as the two girls embraced, then looking at each other to see how a year had changed them.

"You are such a beauty, Genevieve! Your exquisite face and hair, your pretty petite figure."

"You mustn't say such things, Delphine. Beauty is a curse. You will see how ill my beauty serves me, feeding the interest of a man like Robert!"

Delphine's looks on the other hand had not improved with age. She was still pale, her overbite more pronounced and though she had the beautiful light blue eyes of her mother, her blonde hair was thin and wispy. None-the-less, she exuded a gentleness that was appealing.

Genevieve took her hand and they walked into the warmth of the chateau up to her bedchamber. Genevieve stoked the fire to warm Delphine after her long trip. Delphine's hands were like ice in Genevieve's. She rubbed them to warm them for her and brought a chair close to the fire.

"So Delphine, tell me any news, happy news. I need happy news."

"Happy news? Well, you are in luck. I have a young man! He is a simple man, he lives on the neighboring land on his father's farm, a huge farm. They are comfortably off so he can marry when he wishes. I believe he wants to marry me when I am a bit older. His name is Etienne and like me, he is blonde and blue-eyed. We would have such lovely children!" Delphine rambled on about her new love and it brought much joy to Genevieve to know her friend would always be loved and cared for.

But the mood got suddenly serious when Delphine asked after Genevieve. Genevieve was uncertain what to tell her. She didn't want to shock her but she needed someone to talk to. She began telling her that she had gotten her woman's blood and that now she would be expected to perform her wifely duties and bear a child.

"Oh, you poor dear, what did the midwife say?!"

"She had said I wouldn't be ready till my hips grow farther apart. I still have a boyish figure but I doubt that will stop Robert!" and before she could stop herself, she burst into tears and told Delphine about her night with the two women in Robert's room

Delphine was visibly shaken and shuddered as a chill went up her spine. She felt faint and ill. Gently she took Genevieve in her arms.

"This is unacceptable, you must leave him! He is a monster. You must come away with me right away. Quick, pack your bags and we will leave at once!" Delphine said with urgency.

In a daze and slightly exuberant at the thought of escape, she packed a few precious belongings and they raced to the stables. The carriage was made ready with fresh horses from the chateau and off they went with instructions to the driver to continue through the night until they were back at Delphine's house. The girls held hands in fear and excitement.

It being winter, the carriage was very cold. The girls huddled under the blankets but after a time, it just wasn't enough. When they should have stopped to warm up, they continued on in order to arrive at Delphine's before Robert discovered her disappearance. The dark arrived and the temperature dropped further. Seeing that Delphine was shivering, she wrapped all the blankets around her and instructed the driver to stop at the first inn or ale house they came to.

She knew that a delay would be fatal to her escape but she felt Delphine's health was in jeopardy.

When they stopped, Genevieve asked the driver to escort them into the inn for their safety and so he might warm up too. Once inside, they settled as close to the fire as possible. Genevieve ordered mulled wine for Delphine and was handing it to her when a commotion occurred at the door.

"I'm looking for my wife, is she here?" a voice shouted. Genevieve's blood ran cold. It was Robert. They should have hidden the carriage out back. What could she do now? She hastily passed the cup to Delphine and ran to hide but it was too late. He's seen her and was making his way to her side.

"Where do you think you are going without my permission? How dare you take it upon yourself to go on a trip without consulting me! Come with me."

He had grabbed her arm and continued to hold her. Delphine was standing, flushed and shivering.

"Delphine, I must go back but I beg of you, stay here for the night so you don't get more chilled. It's dangerous for you!" Genevieve pleaded.

Delphine was speechless. She was terrified of Robert and collapsed back into her chair crying.

Robert dragged Genevieve out to his horse and pushed her in front of him. Angrily, he whipped the horse into motion. It galloped along for a couple of miles and just as Genevieve thought she would die of the cold, Robert stopped at an inn and pulled her inside with him. He asked for a room for the night and the innkeeper, flattered that such a gentleman was on his premises, showed them up to his bed room. It had its own fireplace and a four-poster bed with red curtains. Genevieve sat in a chair awaiting Robert's wrath.

"I will deal with you later. Right now, we must warm up and eat something so move that chair by the fire," he said in hushed tones. She did as she was told, grateful that she wasn't going to be punished, at least for now.

After a dinner that included a lot of mulled wine, Genevieve felt numb with exhaustion and despair. Robert decided it was time for bed and ordered her to get out of her dress and under the covers. Genevieve was grateful for the warmth of the bed but worried about sharing the bed with Robert. He took a while to finish his wine and undress before he climbed in beside her. She feigned sleep. To her dismay, she sensed he was naked and from the smell of him, drunk. He lay down beside her and pulled her to him.

"Stop Robert, what are you doing?!"

"Doing? You dare to tell me to stop? Who do you think you are? I'll tell you. You are my wife in the eyes of the law and in the eyes of God, and damn it, you will be my wife in all ways. I'm tired of this charade and of waiting!"

He threw himself on top of her and tried to kiss her but she shook her head back and forth to avoid his lips. Finally, he grabbed her by the waist and flipped her over, pressing her face into the pillow to muffle any scream sound she might make. Pulling up her chemise, he proceeded with his intention of satisfying his lust.

Genevieve jerked in a spasm of pain when he tried and gave a muffled cry. Attempting without success several times, he finally gave up and flopped down on the bed.

Weeping silently, she gasped for breath and crawled out of the bed. There was a burning and sharp pain between her legs and she hobbled over to the chair by the fire. Humiliated and hurting, she clenched her fists in anger and slowly paced her hands between her legs to ease the pain. Blood showed on her chemise but she was too upset to care.

The next day Robert awoke to find Genevieve asleep in the chair. When he noticed the blood on her chemise, he felt slightly chagrined about his behavior of the night before. But he reminded himself that she was his wife and he was entitled to have his way with her. He realized that several hours in the saddle might be painful to her so he paid for an extra blanket for her to fold up and sit on as they rode back to the chateau.

Once Robert and Genevieve arrived home, Robert pushed her into her room and locked the door. The next day he sent for the midwife to have her reappraise Genevieve's physical condition as a woman.

"I've been patient way too long! I'm tired of waiting! It's been over a year and I have not consummated my marriage. You better prepare her because by the end of this week, she will be mine in all senses of the word."

He slammed the door closing Madame Therese and Genevieve in.

"Well, my dear, I'm afraid we can't put this off any longer. You have the oils and salves that you must apply every night this week. Yes, the first few times will be painful but your body will adjust to accommodate him."

Chapter Three

G enevieve did as Madame Therese had told her, desperately trying to be prepared for the inevitable. The week passed by, and the night came when Robert expected her in his bed. Dinner dragged on in slow motion as she waited with dread for evening to fall. He finally gulped down his last drink and bringing the bottle with him, took her by the arm and led her to his room.

"Take your clothes off and get in the bed," he ordered.

She slowly undid her gown, folding it neatly and placing it on a chair, drawing out her undressing as long as possible. Then, still in her chemise, she crawled under the covers and lay looking away from him as he threw his clothes on the floor and clambered into bed.

"Are you in your chemise? I told you to take your clothes off!"

Under the covers, she pulled off her chemise and lay down with her back to him. She saw the vials of the oils and salves on the table by the bed. Who had put them there? Did everyone know that tonight was the night she would lose her virginity? She blushed in humiliation.

As he started to caress her, she reminded him of the oils and salves.

"Put some on you," he stated. "And hurry up and don't forget to put some on me."

When she was done, she told him she was ready. He quickly clambered on top of her. She turned her face away from his and gritted her teeth. It was excruciating for her in spite of all her preparation. She counted the seconds it took him to be done. Finally, he rolled away and she curled up in a ball, holding herself between her legs. As the midwife had warned her, blood appeared on her hands and the sheet.

"Can I go now?" she whispered

"Go? Now? No, I might want you again."

The thought had never crossed her mind.

"But I'm in so much pain. Can we wait for another night to do this again?" she asked tentatively.

"Well, since it's your first time, I guess so," he conceded.

Gratefully, she crawled out of the bed. Quickly putting on her chemise, she gathered up her clothes and staggered from the room. In the privacy of her own room, she gently washed herself, and placing a towel between her legs, she lay down with hopes of falling asleep, but she spent a restless night full of nightmares reliving her humiliation and pain.

Every other night that week, Robert insisted on her attending to his physical needs. It gave her just enough time for the pain to go away before it was inflicted upon her again. She was grateful at least for that. Genevieve most hated the moments when her husband was almost done. His moment of total vulnerability repulsed her even more than his sexual savagery. It always reminded her that there was a moment when she was stronger, enough to kill him. And it brought home to her that she didn't have the courage to do it. Therefore, it meant that in some way, she found life with him tolerable, that she agreed on some level, even allowed it. It always filled her with self-loathing.

The midwife's salves and oils had helped a little but not enough. When she had visited, Madame Therese had said that it was to be expected. After all, she was a wee girl of thirteen with a husband of thirty, a big man at that.

"All that's left is for us to pray to the Mother, that he keels over and dies from all his drinking before he kills you, my dear. It's a sin against the Goddess this marriage, and most certainly a sin against nature. When I go home after seeing you and what he does to your poor little body, it's all I can do to eat my dinner!" Therese said.

Genevieve learned to live with it. She knew the arrangement: as soon as she became with child, he'd promised the midwife he would leave her alone "for the baby's sake." So as much as she dreaded her physical encounters with him, she knew it was her path to freedom.

The night came when Robert declared he was bored with her.

They sat at dinner and Robert idly twirled his wine glass.

"I'm so bored," he drawled. "Being with you in the bed is beyond dull. All you do is lie there like a dead fish. What's the point? Aren't you with child yet?"

Genevieve blushed but secretly she thought her prayers had been answered.

Chapter Four

It was a week later that a messenger on horseback came to the chateau. Genevieve was summoned to the Great Hall where Robert stood with the messenger by the fire. As Genevieve came closer, she saw a look of anger on Robert's face. Why the messenger? she thought.

"Genevieve, this man has come from Viscount Bruneau with a message only for you. I am rather annoyed that he hasn't shared it with me as your husband, but he claims he made a promise to speak directly to you."

"What is it? How are they? Why have you come? Is Delphine engaged to be married?" she asked.

The messenger replied, "Engaged? No, she was very ill when she returned home from her visit with you. She caught a chill and was soon laid down with such a sickness. She spoke your name many times in her delirium. Viscount Bruneau had every doctor and healer come but it was no use. She will die soon but he wants you to see her before she goes to God. She loves you so, like a sister, he says. The viscount needs you too. He will need your comfort when she is gone."

Genevieve fell to her knees and wept. She had to go immediately. She pulled herself together and rose, telling the messenger, "I'll be ready in a minute! Wait for me!"

She raced off to her room to pack a small bag but before she was finished, Robert was in her room.

"Why are you here? I must pack and go with him at once!"

"He is gone. I sent him away. You may not go to see them. She is the enemy. She tried to help you escape, to leave me! I'm glad she will be dead and never able to help you again!"

Genevieve could not believe her ears. She ran to the door shouting, "Stop, wait, I'm coming!"

Robert grabbed her but she turned and bit his arm. "How could you?! How could you!? You are a monster, a heartless monster!" she cried.

Pushing passed him, she raced to the stables. "Hurry up, saddle up Chestnut right now!" she screamed at the groom. "Hurry, please, I must get out of here!"

But before she could make her escape, Robert was there. He grabbed her and flung her down. Grabbing the whip that stood against the wall, he struck her repeatedly on the back. Her dress tore open with each lash and blood pooled on her back. Weeping in pain and rage, she struggled to her feet.

Robert dragged her back to the chateau and up into her room. She gathered up enough strength to fly at him, scratching and biting in her desperation. He held her arms away from him and flung her on the bed. He slid out of the room quickly and she heard the key in the lock.

Genevieve's rage and sorrow about losing Delphine and not having a chance to say good-bye knew no bounds. She pounded on her door until her fists were too bruised to continue. Then she kicked and kicked, and her will finally broken, she lay on her bed and wept. Thoughts continued to race in Genevieve's head. That she would never see her beloved Delphine again and that Delphine would never have her happy marriage to Etienne and the beautiful children she so wanted! And all because of Delphine's devotion. She had come to comfort her and risked her life, no, lost her life in the process! Genevieve's guilt gnawed at her, and jumping up from her bed, she paced the room back and forth, back and forth wondering what she could do.

"Delphine, my beloved Delphine, please know that I wanted to come to you but Robert has locked me in my room and left me here! I love you so much and would do anything for you! Please don't die! Etienne needs you. Your father needs you. I don't deserve you but I too need you. Please God, spare her life. Take mine instead. I am less worthy and have less to lose. Please!!!"

After many hours, night fell and Genevieve realized there was nothing she could do. Robert had not come back, even to give her supper so she had no means of trying to convince him to let her go.

In such turmoil, Genevieve had been barely aware of the state of her back. Unwashed and untended, the cuts would begin to fester. She knew she should be seen by the doctor, but there was nothing she could do.

It wasn't until several days later that Robert released her from her room. She realized what this meant. Delphine was dead. The viscount had sent word that Delphine had slipped into unconsciousness and died within the same day.

Robert showed no remorse for keeping her confined but he was shocked by the condition of her back. Too embarrassed to send for the doctor, he sent for Madame Therese and threatened that she better hold her tongue or else.

Therese was shocked by the state of Genevieve's back and disgusted by Robert's cruelty. She gently washed each cut with warm water until they were thoroughly clean and then put salves on the open wounds. Carefully she bandaged her back and said she would return daily until they were healed.

After a week, the sores had formed scabs and she was able to dress properly.

"I'm afraid you will have scars, my dear, but no one will see them except Robert and it might make him think twice to control his rage!"

That Sunday Genevieve lit a candle for her departed friend and went to confession with a heavy heart.

"Father, I have continued to sin. I have wished my husband dead a thousand times."

"Why, my child?"

"He has treated me ill. He has humiliated me, he has beaten me so I will have scars on my back but worst of all, he has denied me my final chance to be with my dear Delphine when she was dying! He is a cruel monster and tortures me physically and emotionally. I only wish for his death!"

"My child, I have to confess that Therese told me of your beating. I did not know of all the other situations but they are disgraceful and sins against you and against God. I think it is time for you to leave your husband. I do not say this lightly. I have been thinking of you and your predicament for a long time and I have come up with a plan. Listen carefully. I am close friends with the abbot at Saint Grieff. His monastery is a couple of days ride from here. I have told Father Bernard that a young boy needs a home away from an abusive father. He has said he would give safe harbor to this boy. Do you see what I am getting at?"

"A boy at Saint Grieff? No, Father, what do you mean?"

"You are young, and barely a woman. If you cut your hair, bind your breasts and dress in boy's clothes, you could pass for a boy. Robert would never think of looking for you there. You would finally be safe and under the protection of God."

"A boy, me? Could I really? …Anything would be better than life with Robert. Now I have so much to plan and think about!"

"God bless you, my child!"

Genevieve left the confessional in a daze. Could she do it, free herself from Robert, live as a boy?

When she got home, she looked in her mirror and imagined herself as a boy. Yes, she might be able to do it. With growing excitement, she planned her escape.

That evening Robert asked her why she had been in the confessional for so long. "What sins have you committed that needed forgiveness? As your husband, I demand to know."

"What sins have I committed? Nothing compared to you and yet you never go to confession. Perhaps you know your soul is damned already. At least in death I will be free of you. You are sure to go to hell!" Genevieve spat out the words and saw the dark anger fill Robert's blue eyes.

"How dare you speak to me that way! Come here and beg my forgiveness immediately."

"No! Never, you should be begging my forgiveness! Every Sunday I go to confession and am forgiven for my sins. And do you know what my sin is? That I pray every night for your death! That is my sin!"

Robert stood shocked by her confession. Visibly shaking with rage, he slapped her across the face, sending her to the floor. She tried to scramble back on her feet but before she could, he gave her a vicious kick and then pulled her up to her feet. Grabbing both her arms, he lifted her off the floor and threw her against the wall. She fell into a slump on the floor unconscious.

Robert called his man servants to carry her to her room. He did not bother to call the doctor. Instead, he had a maid servant care for her with instructions to tell him the moment she woke up.

The next day, Genevieve woke, bruised and aching. Her head spun and waves of nausea overcame her when she tried to sit up. The maid rushed from the room to alert Robert.

Slowly Genevieve raised herself up. Her arms were bruised where Robert had grabbed her and her face still hurt. Her mouth tasted of blood. She slowly walked to the mirror to see what her face looked like. Her lower lip had a deep cut and was swollen. Her nose was bruised as was her left eye. She looked terrible. How could she go out looking like this? The shame of having angered her husband so consumed her. Why had she told him that? Why hadn't she kept her mouth shut? She knew he was angry when she first looked into his eyes and yet she continued to taunt him.

Just then Robert entered the room.

"Get back in bed. You are not well. That fall you took down the stairs has really knocked up your face and head. You must rest," he said in front of the maid. But when she turned her back, Robert gripped her arm and whispered. "I'm not through with you yet!"

That Sunday Robert did not allow her to go to church because her face was still bruised. Pere LeMaitre asked after her, hiding his worry, and Robert told him with feigned concern that she had had a spill down the stairs and was too embarrassed to show up at church with her bruises. Pere LeMaitre concealed his alarm and simply said "Wish her well from me."

"I will, Father." Robert replied and rode off.

The following Sunday, Genevieve's bruises had faded enough that Robert allowed her to go to church. She sat in great discomfort on the pews next to Robert and repeated silently to herself over and over: "I have had enough. I have had enough!".

When it came time for confession, Genevieve's heart gave a leap and she hurried into the confessional.

"Father, I have sinned."

"Genevieve, I understand you were hurt. Was that Robert's doing?"

"Yes, he threw me against a wall and I was unconscious. He would not let me come last Sunday because my face was cut and bruised where he hit me."

"I suspected as much. Very well. I will give you a map and a set of boy's clothes but I must leave them at the stone by the crossroads.

I don't dare have you seen talking to me because Robert will know it was me who helped you. He is sure to try to get the information out of me. So, I will leave a package for you tonight and you may choose the time you wish to leave. It should be about a two days ride from here if you rest during the night. Do you understand?"

"Yes Father, thank you so much. Thank you and bless you!" "Go with God, my child!"

Though she still hurt, Genevieve waited until midnight and taking nothing with her, she fled to the stable, quietly saddled up Chestnut, and off she raced. At the cross roads, she quickly tethered Chestnut and found the package behind the rock as Pere LeMaitre had said she would. She ran into the woods and threw off all her clothes. There was a bandage for her to bind her breasts and then the roughest of boy's garments. There was also a knife for her to cut off her long locks, and to protect herself if needed. With a moment of regret, she chopped away at her beautiful auburn locks and bound the remainder back with a piece of rope. Gathering up any evidence of her existence, she placed her clothes and hair in her satchel, ran back to Chestnut and continued on her way in the darkness of night.

PART THREE:
Monastery

Chapter One

Genevieve's first night was filled with a mixture of profound relief and sorrow. The obvious sense of relief was that her arduous journey was now over and that she was safe from her husband. She would be able to put the endless gnawing fear behind her and perhaps sleep in peace unless she was haunted by him in her dreams. At least those she would wake from with a sigh of relief, unlike the living nightmares she experienced sleeping under his roof.

Her fear now was that she would be discovered in this masquerade and only God would know what would happen to her then. Father Bernard had seemed so warm and understanding when she arrived with the letter of introduction from Pere LeMaitre. Tears of relief and gratitude had begun to form in her eyes at his warmth but she pulled herself together, remembering that she could never let herself fall apart living here as she was disguised as a young boy.

"You will be up in the tower in the cell next to Brother Evechio, as that is all there is available. It is one of the coldest locations in the monastery but you are as young and strong as he is, so it is better that you be there than one of the older monks. Brother Evechio is a novice and seventeen years of age. He works in the scriptorium on manuscripts and illuminations. You, on the other hand, will be working in the kitchen. Be grateful. It is one of the warmest places in the monastery. I have asked Brother Evechio to take you under his wing."

Again, he smiled kindly and Genevieve quickly leaned over and kissed his hand in gratitude before she was ushered out and led to her room.

True to his word, her cell at the top of the tower was freezing. All the room contained was bedding with several wool blankets (thank God for that), a pitcher and basin for washing, and a rough sponge. Her life as the adopted daughter of a viscount and wife of a lord had taught her to love the luxuries of life but the first eight years with her artisan father in their simple abode had made the roughness of the voyage and austerity of the monastery just bearable.

Two slivers of windows faced each other on each side of the tower. A wooden door stood at one end of the cell and a wooden ladder stood on the other side, leading up to the roof where a trap door rested closed. Perhaps it led to a store room but judging from the cold, it led directly to the roof of the tower.

Looking around, she thought how dreary and empty, cold and austere this place was. The bell for morning service would ring at dawn whether she was ready or not and she was exhausted from her journey. But what else was there to do in this desolate place? What did the monks do in the evenings when they were through with their religious devotions? She had no art supplies, no embroidery threads, no books, no games, no one to write a letter to and no one to talk to. Nothing and no one left in all the world.

The energy she had spent in running in terror was no longer needed and was replaced with an enormous sense of all she had lost, and the immensity of her sorrow and aloneness. What of Robert's anger at her deception? Would he blame Pere LeMaitre and the Viscount Bruneau? If she thought they would be punished for her behavior, she might have suffered longer at Robert's hands. She shook the thought from her mind. What's done is done. But what was her life worth now, living hidden as a monk in a bleak monastery worshipping a God she barely believed in and didn't love. Thoughts spun in her mind a mile a minute as the tears streamed down her dusty and weary face.

Too agitated to sleep, she decided to climb the ladder and look at the night stars until peace would come to her. The night sky was dark and the stars twinkled brilliantly in the frigid air. Though her robe was made of wool, she shivered. She felt feverish though and a huge wave of heat deadened her mind. Her thoughts seemed to melt and her sorrow enveloped her. She couldn't bear her life. Death and misery surrounded her wherever she went. That she had caused Delphine's death meant she would forever hate herself. Why had she been saved when so many others had died? Why was God tormenting her, if there was a God? What was he saving her for? What future miseries and torments? If anything, she believed in the devil, not God.

She couldn't bear the thought of a life of constant pain and guilt; it was so intense she choked on it. She suddenly realized what she must do, what she should have done long ago before putting others at risk. Slowly she stepped up onto the bench that rested against the tower wall, as though her entire body was in tune with what her mind told her to do. She stood feeling the wind and put her frigid hands together.

"My dearest mother, who I know so little, please forgive me for giving up this life you gave me. Please welcome me with open arms and I hope God will let me join you! My dearest Delphine, forgive me for robbing you of a life full of love and the chance to have the children you always wanted. Please, please, forgive me that the disaster that is my life led to your death. It is I who should have died, I, who was too much of a coward to stand up for myself! That you are safe in Heaven is my only consolation. And finally, my dearest, dearest father, this is my last prayer to you!" Genevieve laughed a little at the irony of it and thought of the joy of finally being with him again after all these years.

"In a minute now, I will not have to pray to you anymore. Instead, I will be right there by your side. As you promised me, to keep me close and safe eternally! So, my dearest Papa, be sure to be there to greet me with your open arms. I love you."

She now began to hoist her light frame onto the thick heavy stonework. She worried that she might not be able to join her loved ones in Heaven immediately because of her sinfulness but she hoped one day, after she paid for her sins in purgatory, she would.

Suddenly she felt a warm hand on hers and heard a gentle voice. As if in a fog, she lost track of where she was. Where was the voice coming from? Who was there? Had she jumped? Was it all over? Could it really have been that painless? She smiled.

"You are smiling. I am glad you feel like smiling".

The voice spoke slowly and softly and arms encircled her waist.

"Can I ask you why you are smiling? "

"Am I dead? Is it always this painless to die?"

"Dead? …That's what you wanted to be, to be dead? Are you so sure that's where you should be?"

"Of course, it is the best idea, I will cease to hurt others…If I am dead, won't I become an angel and be able to do nothing but help others? Won't I…?"

Gently, the arms encircled her.

"You say you want to help others? You can do that here on earth. We all need so much help here on earth in so many ways, and so many people, children, the old, the poor, the sick, the lonely, those who need to learn compassion and love…to continue all the loving work Jesus taught us… Yes, you can even be a stronger angel by living and suffering on earth in order to help others. Death is selfish, it's the easy way out, don't you see that?"

"Selfish, easy? … Yes I see… I see… Of course you are right!"

In her excitement, Genevieve began to be loosened out of her trance and its emotional numbness. Suddenly the whole world seemed to crash in on her with an emotional intensity she had never experienced before, as if all the emotions and pain she had hoped to escape by her death were pressing in on her a thousandfold.

"Oh my God! Oh my God, what have I done?"

In her agony, she crumpled and fell in whatever direction her body took her. But arms held her tight and carried her from the ramparts...her angel, she thought, her angel.

"My angel, who are you...who are you?"

"We'll worry about that later. Right now, I have to get you downstairs into a warm bed. You are in shock and absolutely frozen. The wind tonight is frightful! Introductions will come later."

Carefully he clambered down the ladder clutching her in his arms. Her head lay against his shoulder and she could hear his labored breathing and feel its warmth upon her face. The glorious warmth of his entire body where she was pressed against it was all that she could focus on. She shivered and clung closer to him when they reached her bed and he tried to release her.

"No angel, ...please, my angel...don't leave me...I'm so cold and so alone."

"Of course, I'm not leaving you. You need help right now. I'm going to be looking over you for a long time, so you better get used to it. I guess I am your angel, your guardian angel, you poor lost little boy! You need warmth and sleep. Now under the covers with you."

He lifted the blankets and laid her down, but she couldn't bear the freezing cold.

Shivering she cried out: "Please don't go! Please don't leave me!"

"Petit Jean, that's your name, isn't it? I am going nowhere! So move over because if I am staying by your side for the night, I am not going to be so foolish as to freeze outside the covers! What help would I be to you then?!"

He laughed a deep warm laugh and before she could say another word, he leapt under the covers, holding her to bring warmth back to her freezing body. Surrounded by the security and warmth of his presence and exhausted by all that had happened, she closed her eyes in resignation and delirium and fell into a deep sleep.

Chapter Two

Genevieve woke to the sound of a distant ringing. She heard it coming closer and she slowly opened her eyes. Where was she? She had a vague recollection of her flight but now she realized she was still at the monastery and on her palette. It was still dark out and she remembered that Father Bernard had said they awakened at four.

She groaned inwardly and was about to drag herself out of her bed when she heard a voice groggily say: "Good morning, Jean, how are you feeling today?"

Genevieve turned swiftly around and gave a slight scream. She pulled the covers to her chin, even though she was covered by her robe, and wondered what on earth she should do or say. It was too dark to see her companion at all clearly. But his accented voice was deep and rich.

"Hello, it's me, your angel, Brother Evechio. At least you called me your angel last night. I gather you must have been a bit delirious and don't remember everything? You needed a lot of help last night and that's what I did. Are you feeling better?"

Genevieve's memory began to clear: the tower, he saved her from that fatal mistake.

"My angel. Yes, I remember and I thank you a hundred times over but what are you doing in my bed?"

"Trying to get you warmed up. You begged me to stay so I obliged. You were in very bad shape and I have been instructed to take you under my wing. No more bad thoughts, I hope? Otherwise, I will have to watch you carefully."

"I see. Those bad thoughts should be gone now I am safely here. I ran away from a very brutal…" She stopped to think, "…father. But that is all over now!"

"Good, I'm glad to hear you feel better. Now splash some water on your face and put on your sandals and then we go to morning service. I'll show you the way."

He scrambled out of the bed and went to the cell next door, the other half of the tower. She quickly scurried to her feet, washed her face and searched in the dark for her sandals. Evechio returned with a hair brush.

"You better brush that tangle of yours!"

She took it gratefully, untied her hair and brushed. The tangles took a while but she managed to make it tidy and tie it back again. He remained a shadowy figure in the dark and she wondered what the person looked like who had such a melodic voice.

Evechio led her down some stone steps and through the silent halls. Other monks were appearing from their cells and walking rapidly towards the stairs. There was some coughing but no sounds other than that.

The final walk was in the freezing outside as they made their way down a flag stone path to the side entrance of the church. Evechio gave a slight bow of his head at the door with his palms together and then did the signs of the cross on his person: Father, Son and Holy Ghost, head, chest, shoulder, shoulder. So far so good. Genevieve was familiar with all this because of her studies with Pere LeMaitre and her attendance at church. Evechio took his place on a pew near the back of the church and immediately knelt in prayer. She knelt beside him, grimacing at the cold hard stone against her knees. The prayers seemed to go on and on. She thought she should try to pray too.

"Thank you, Lord, for my safety and my new life. Thank you for Pere LeMaitre and Father Bernard, and thank you for my new friend, Brother Evechio. She glanced over at him as he knelt in prayer and wished she could see him clearly.

The service progressed and Genevieve was pleased that she could follow along because of the services she had attended at Pere LeMaitre's church. She remembered when to stand, to kneel, to make the signs of the cross.

Evechio glanced over several times to make sure she was following along and soon stopped as he realized she knew what to do. The service went on a long time and Genevieve's mind began to wander:

Who is this shadowy figure next to me? Evechio, she said to herself. What a strange name. She must ask him about it. She blushed when she remembered they had slept in the same bed. Little did he know that he had been sleeping with a girl! Would he be horrified? It was lucky they slept in their robes!

As the service ended, chanting filled the church. Genevieve found the music beautifully inspiring and it was when she felt closest to God. She shivered and Evechio glanced her way. She was smiling in absolute gratitude for such beauty. She could have stayed there forever enveloped in the sound.

All too soon it was time for communion. Single file, the monks walked up the center aisle to receive the host. When Evechio stood up, she followed. Still, she could not see his face but she could see how smoothly he walked and how straight was his back. He was not a tall man but he had an attractive slim build. She could tell by his shoulder and waist

As they approached the front of the church, a faint candlelight fell upon them. Evechio knelt and motioned for her to kneel beside him. Genevieve kept her head humbly bent down until Father

Bernard came to her with the host. She raised her face with her eyes closed and took the host into her mouth. Slowly the wafer dissolved on her tongue, and then came the wine. The body and blood of Christ. What a mystery to her.

Evechio stood up and she did the same. For a moment she glanced at him, this mysterious stranger. The candlelight caressed his strong face and Genevieve was taken aback by the beauty of his profile. A strong chin, defined lips, an aristocratic nose, but his eyes, she wanted to see his eyes. He must have noticed her scrutinizing him, for he turned to look at her. His eyes were a wonderful dark brown, deep pools of mystery. Genevieve took a deep breath and immediately lowered her eyes blushing. What had he thought of her curiosity? She hoped it didn't bother him.

They all filed back to the pews for a last round of prayers and then rose to leave the church. She dutifully followed Evechio, the last one in line due to her status as the newest novice. That meant Evechio was one of the newer monks too. She wondered how long he had been at the monastery.

They entered a large room filled with refectory tables and benches. The smell of warm oatmeal filled the air. Her stomach grumbled in anticipation. Her seat was at the end of one of the tables. In silence, the serving bowl full of oatmeal was passed down the table and each monk helped himself. When it reached her, there was still plenty left. The oatmeal was followed by a bowl of raisins and a small pitcher of honey. Then a pitcher of warm milk. She was beyond grateful.

After the silent meal, a small bucket of hot water was sent down the table. The monks dipped their bowls and spoons in the bucket and removed them, wiping them dry with their cloths. Then they placed them back on the table in front of them. Genevieve grimaced at the thought of cleaning her bowl in used water and not cleaning it properly. And now her cloth was damp. After a bell rang and some chanting of gratitude took place, the abbot stood.

"Work practice for today: those who work in the scriptorium will continue their work. Those who weave and sew will continue with our spring robes."

The list of jobs went on and she wondered what her work would be.

"There is nothing new to report other than the arrival of our youngest monk to be, Brother Jean. Jean, please stand up."

Genevieve turned bright pink at being called out in front of all the monks but she did as she was told, holding her hands before her and looking bravely at Father Bernard. He smiled at her kindly and she felt much relieved.

"I trust you all will help Jean learn our ways and help him where you can. You may sit, Jean"

"Thank you, Father," she squeaked and quickly sat down.

"Now is there anyone who needs to share something?" Father Bernard said glancing at the monk at his side.

The monk bowed his head followed by the monk next to him and several more, until it came to one monk who spoke.

"We need to go to the town for supplies in the next couple of days." Father Bernard bowed. The next monk to speak said:

"We have enough firewood for the kitchen to last four more weeks. I will tell you when we start to run out."

And so, on it went. It finally came to Genevieve and she bowed her head hastily.

Father Bernard rang a small bell and more prayers were said. Finally, the monks rose from their seats and began talking to each other informally about the day's work.

A rotund monk approached Genevieve and said, "Brother Jean, you will be working in the kitchen so come with me."

She followed as he waddled through a door at the side of the dining hall. Genevieve was suddenly enveloped in warmth for the first time since her arrival and she reveled in it. Her spirits rose. She also was greeted by the wonderful aromas of baking bread.

All her fears seemed to dissipate as she moved farther into the kitchen.

"That is your good robe. You need to take one of the robes hanging on the pegs over there and change. I don't want your robe soiled so take it back to your room and hurry. Though we don't allow running. Lesson one: Being quiet is a virtue, remember that."

Genevieve walked as quickly and quietly back to her room, changed and was coming out when she ran into Evechio.

"I'm off to the scriptorium, so I can't help you. Brother Luke, the cook is demanding but jovial so you should do just fine."

Genevieve said good bye and went quickly to the kitchen, again enjoying the enveloping warmth.

Her first chore was to wash the morning dishes, the giant pots and bowls. This was followed by fetching carrots and onions from the cellar and chopping them up for a soup. Brother Luke showed her a quick way to chop the carrots into chunks and she was grateful for his patience. Several of the other monks were busy chopping and stirring and baking. Since she was the youngest, she was the one who was sent scurrying to fetch for the rotund Brother Luke. By noon, when the gong rang, after she had set out the serving bowls on the table, she was told to remove her work robe and change back into her good robes for formal lunch.

Lunch was very much like breakfast, silent and quickly finished. The hearty soup and fresh bread were much to her liking. It reminded her of days with her dear father. The afternoon was spent again in the kitchen and then as the day darkened, the monks were dismissed to dress for evening service and prayers.

By evening, Genevieve was exhausted but her excitement at her new life kept her going. After evening service and prayers, she and Evechio headed up to their rooms. Before he went into his room, Evechio asked her how her first day had been.

"Exhausting but I am happy to be here!"

"I am surprised they have accepted someone so young here. I thought I was young when I came when I was sixteen."

"How long ago was that?"

"One year ago. But it had been decided at my birth that I should go into the monastery.

Maybe one day I will tell you the story of why my life was dedicated to the church at such a young age. And what of you, you told me your father beat you. I can't imagine?"

Genevieve wondered what she should say. She was loathe to lie but now her whole life was a lie.

"Yes, my father beat me often. He was a drinker. My priest was worried for me and arranged for me to come to Mont Grieff. It was kind of Father Bernard to take me in."

"I'm sorry to hear that you've had such a hard time, Jean," Evechio said patting her arm gently. "I hope you find peace here, as I have"

"I can tell that you are not French. Where are you from?" she asked.

"I am from Italy, from the Castel della Felice, in Perugia."

"A castle? Were you wealthy?"

"That's hard to say. Yes, we lived in a castle but with many, many other people. It had been my father's estate at one time. It's a long story and will have to wait for another day, my little friend. It's time we were off to sleep."

He was an interesting man, she thought and she looked forward to getting to know more about him, if he allowed it. Genevieve was sufficiently exhausted that she fell right to sleep in spite of the cold.

Chapter Three

B y the end of the first week, Genevieve was adjusting to the rigors of the schedule, glad that her youth helped her have the necessary energy, and amazed that the older monks could survive so much work on so little sleep. That wasn't to say that each morning, she didn't dread the sound of the ringing bell that told her it was time to wake up. She became an expert at eating quickly, gulping down her milk or broth and shoveling the oatmeal or stew into her mouth unceremoniously. All the monks were trained to keep their eyes down while eating so she was pretty certain no one could see her sloppy manners.

The hours of silence were difficult for her. There were times when she wanted to scream out and release all her tension. Often, she wiggled her toes to relieve the pressure or fidgeted in her seat until she noticed that it drew Evechio's attention away from his prayers. Her favorite time of day was when she first entered the kitchen and was greeted by the warmth and aromas.

Working in the kitchen agreed with her. Though she had no clue how to cook anything, she enjoyed the freedom afforded by the running of errands and the precision of chopping vegetables. She thought, at first, she would find the silent chopping boring, but noticed that she was comfortable with her own thoughts.

Aside from Brother Luke, she slowly got to know a few of the other monks who worked there. Brother Luke's assistant was an older monk, tall, thin and stooped with a long thin face, with pasty white skin and a long, hooked nose. He had old watery eyes and occasionally smiled to himself as he worked. But he never addressed her or looked her way.

The monk who baked bread, on the other hand, was short and slim, with a sensuous mouth and a sparkle in his eyes. He occasionally whispered at Brother Luke which led to laughter. His name was Brother Edward and he often was reading when he had a moment as he waited for his bread to rise.

But of course, her favorite was Evechio. He had totally taken her under his wing. In the evenings when they were not quite so exhausted, they would sit on her bed and talk. He seemed so natural with her and she had to remind herself that he thought of her as a boy. He was a fatherly figure for Genevieve and she found it profoundly comforting. His faith was enormous and she deeply enjoyed hearing about his love of God. It gave her hope that one day she might feel the same way.

One night they were discussing the question of life's difficulties. She said it wasn't fair that people had struggles if God was all powerful. Life should be easy.

"We are not living in heaven yet, petit Jean, we must earn that joy. God is testing us all. Even Jesus, his own son, was sorely tested. But I try to remind myself of what Jesus once said: 'Take up your cross and follow me.' He acknowledged that we all had our trials and suffering to contend with, as he did too. 'Take up your cross...and follow me.' I find such solidarity in those words, such humanity."

Genevieve was moved by Evechio's words. Yes, Jesus had many trials and suffered greatly in his time. God didn't spare him either.

"We are all in it together!" Genevieve responded.

"Exactly, and we can choose to follow the example of Jesus, or go the other way. But isn't it so much better to follow in Jesus' footsteps?"

"Yes, I think you are right. This is the first time I have thought about Jesus, the man, and how he understood us and suffered along with us. I feel a kinship with him!" Genevieve was so pleased to find these feelings in her heart. Perhaps one day she might believe.

Other nights they just discussed the day's happenings, how clumsy Brother Philip knocked over his ink bottle in the scriptorium, or a joke that Brother Edward had told in the kitchen or how Brother Jacob had let the broth boil over. They often laughed at their own errors, especially Genevieve's as she was so new to monastic life. Evechio confessed that he had let the host slip out of his mouth by accident once. Genevieve was secretly horrified but laughed none- the-less.

"And there was the time Brother Jacob sneezed just as the wine chalice was offered to him! No one wanted to drink after that but we had too."

To Genevieve, communion had become the most sacred of acts. She could not imagine talking about it so casually. Even if she didn't believe in the body and blood of Christ, she saw it as the ultimate acknowledgement of the sacrifice Jesus made for humanity and the ultimate way in which to honor him.

Genevieve quickly changed the subject and asked him about his family. He took a deep breath and told her it was a long story, a very long story for another time.

"And what of your family? I gather your father was a horrible man, if you had to escape him."

Genevieve was horrified that she would have to say anything against her father, real or make-believe. Her father had been her champion and they had adored one another. What could she say?

"You have to understand that my father was not always like that. There was a time when I was really young that he adored me, but after my mother died, he took to the drink and began to take his anger and pain out on me."

That was as close to the truth as Genevieve could get. She combined the three men she knew best, for better or for worse, in her story. First her father, then Viscount Bruneau and finally Robert. She shivered as she thought of him and Evechio put his arm around her.

"I'm so sorry that you lost your mother and then lost your father to the drink. It seems to be very common."

Without thinking, Genevieve rested her head on his shoulder as she had so often with her own father.

"You poor little boy. But things are going well for you here so you may decide to take vows and stay! Perhaps you could work in the scriptorium, since you love reading so much." Evechio tousled her hair and smiled down at her. She felt her heart melt a little and quickly sat up.

"Off to sleep with you, we don't want you sleepy and chopping your finger instead of a carrot! Imagine finding a finger in your bowl!"

They both laughed and Evechio took his leave. Genevieve got in bed thoughtfully, revisiting the moment with Evechio that had touched her heart. He was such a good man, and yet so easy to be with and so fun. She was not used to that and she liked it. She went to sleep that night with pleasant thoughts.

Much as Genevieve doted on Evechio, there was one of the other monks that intrigued Genevieve. He was Brother Stephan. Brother Stephan was from England but he spoke French beautifully with a melodic voice. What was even more interesting about him was that he was blind. He had not been blind since birth. Rather he had received a massive blow to the head when he was eighteen that had left him blind. His wealthy family had sent him to the good brothers as soon as they could. Under what circumstances he received the blow were never discussed and Genevieve was too polite to ask.

He was a tall, lanky fellow, scrawny almost with fine long fingers. His face was defined with a thin mouth and a strong elegant nose, and his blind eyes were a beautiful blue. He had gone white in the hair at a young age and Genevieve knew he was only in his thirties. The small pox had left his visage marred in a rugged way that pleased her. On the whole, he was pleasant to look at.

Genevieve had been given the job to read to him each day. Since Genevieve spent a couple of hours a day with Stephan, she had come to respect and enjoy him. He was rather an unusual person, very passive and uncertain due to his infirmity, having not adjusted well to it. He was gentle and sensitive, almost feminine in his sensibilities. Genevieve felt infinitely comfortable with him and was often tempted to confide in him about her sorrows.

Stephan was an accomplished viola player, one of the few pleasures available to him. He played by ear and was quite gifted. His ethereal touch blended perfectly with their spiritual services in church. But often Genevieve came across him playing in the open air in the orchard, far enough away from the monastery in order to not be heard. This was when he played with a passion and force that surprised Genevieve and stirred her blood. How did he know these passionate emotions, this quiet and shy and blind monk? When he played that way, Genevieve quietly left before he knew she was there. She felt she was intruding on something personal and vaguely improper for a monastery. Other days his songs were understandably mournful and haunting. These broke her heart and she interrupted him to give him cheer by her company. Then she would read to him for an extra long time, hoping to distract him from his sorrow.

Chapter Four

One day, as she was secretly listening to Stephan's impassioned music, she tripped on her robe and fell to the ground, giving a shout of surprise and pain.

"Who's there?" called Stephan, abruptly stopping his playing, blushing deeply and with a tone of embarrassment and concern in his voice.

"It is only me. I was in the vegetable garden weeding and heard the far off sounds of your playing. It was so beautiful, I had to hear more. I should go now. I hope that Brother Luke is not looking for me right now." said Genevieve urgently, eager to leave since she had been caught spying on him.

"Oh, Jean, it's you. That's good, yes... good that it is you. I do not like being observed without my knowledge, even after all these years. There are so few times and people to observe me here, it is a comfort. But you must always let me know when you are near. Will you do that for me?"

"Yes, Brother Stephan, I will do that. It is the least I can do. You do not mind me listening to your playing? I have such lovely memories of music from my childhood...before my father took to drink," she added hastily. She had to keep up her pretense and her story with everyone, everyone including Brother Stephan and Brother Evechio, the two hardest to keep deceiving.

After renewing her promise to Stephan, Genevieve ran back to the garden to continue weeding, hoping that her disappearance hadn't been noticed.

Unfortunately, that was not the case. Brother Luke stood at the kitchen door, hands on his ample hips, with a sour expression on his face.

"Where have you been, you good for nothing scoundrel? Resting your buttocks somewhere? Day dreaming as you always do. If you weren't so young and scrawny, I would punish you, but you would like as die if I struck you or withheld your meals for a day. Now hurry up and get me some leeks for our luncheon!" Brother Luke ranted, though not completely unkindly. Genevieve looked chagrined and raced to pull up the leeks as quickly as she could.

When she brought them to Brother Luke, he gave her a half-hearted cuff to the head and grabbed them roughly from her hands.

"Now back out to the weeding and don't let me catch you wandering off again! I want that row of carrots weeded before lunch."

"Absolutely, Brother Luke. I promise" replied Genevieve and she focused all her energies on the weeding, pushing the impassioned music she had heard to the back of her mind.

After she had made good progress, she allowed her mind to wander back to Brother Stephan and his music. He must know a lot more about life than he lets on, she thought. Such passion! What could he have had to be passionate about? She continued in her musing. A girl? Brother Stephan? Genevieve just couldn't imagine it. He lacked manliness in the way to which she was accustomed. He was an enigma, and her curiosity was sorely roused. One day she would ask him, she promised herself.

She herself had never felt passion, only terror when it came to the desires of her husband. Yet Stephan's music spoke of a passion that was beautiful. Would she ever know about that passion? How long would she be staying here at the monastery? Months, years?

Would she end up in a nunnery one day? She had no options. She was completely at Father Bernard's mercy.

Her life literally depended on him. It was a good thing that she felt confident about him. Imagine if she always was on pins and needles, wondering if she was to be tossed out on the street. She had best do her most at all times to impress him with her work ethic and spiritual devotion. With that thought in her mind, she resumed her ardent weeding of the garden.

Genevieve knew that Brother Stephan was the only son from a good family. He should have inherited the wealth and been set for life, so it didn't make sense that he should have been sent to a monastery. That was usually the fate of the second son, the third being sent to join the army. That he was blind was not a good enough reason to banish him from his home, life of privilege, and his title. Genevieve's concern for Brother Stephan and her curiosity about his singular person and situation worked on her.

The day finally came when Stephan told Genevieve his story. They were sitting in the orchard one spring day, reading a text by Plato. Genevieve was very intrigued by his ideas about love and enjoyed reading those passages even though they were not pertinent to the spiritual life of a monk.

The breeze murmured through the trees and the apple blossoms fluttered around them. Stephan took a deep breath of the sweet scent of the flowers and suddenly put his hand out, signaling to stop reading. Curious, Genevieve looked up into his face and saw tears in his eyes.

"Brother Stephan, are you alright? Have I displeased you with my reading?"

"No Jean, not at all. I am deeply moved by your reading and Plato's ideas of love. The smell of the blossoms and this time of year are bringing back memories of long ago, the best day of my life and the worst!"

"The best and the worst? How can that be?"

"I think it is time for me to tell my story. I have never told anyone and you must never breath a word of it to anyone, do you understand?"

Intrigued and honored that he would choose her to confide in, she assured him she would never betray his confidences.

STEPHAN'S STORY

Yes, he was the only son of an Earl. He was entitled to great wealth and comfort but on many levels, he dissatisfied his father. For one, he couldn't bear the hunt, seeing animals so brutally killed by his father's hounds. After a point. he refused to go.

But the real trouble began when he discovered the viola and the pleasures of music. It was not that his father objected to his learning an instrument. It was the trouble that came later. His mother hired a music teacher for Stephan when she realized how talented he was. Stephan was fifteen at the time and his tutor, Michael, was but a few years older. Stephan's passion for music grew under the tutelage of the new music teacher. It seemed that Stephan couldn't get enough. Lessons became more frequent and longer and his admiration and attachment to Michael grew. Stephan felt Michael was the only person who understood him. He spent many hours telling him his hopes and dreams.

Before he knew it, he found that he cherished Michael in a way he had never cherished anyone before. And his body responded in suit. That was the most troubling part for Stephan.

They would be playing a duet and Stephan would see how the sunlight fell upon Michael's hair and he grew absent-minded with the desire to caress Michael's golden curls. He would skip a note. Or he would grow faint at the proximity of Michael's body when he would come behind him to adjust his posture. He would break into a sweat with the fear that Michael would notice. What would he say? Would he be horrified and depart, to be lost forever? God forbid anyone find out.

But one day, his secret desire could be contained no longer. It began with a conversation about his love of music.

"I know I am lucky to be born into this family of wealth, but if I could, I would travel the country as a troubadour, going down the open road, playing for my supper. What do you think of that?" Stephan told Michael wistfully.

"It's an exciting life to be sure, but it wears thin very quickly. I can't tell you how grateful I am for a roof over my head and meals every day."

"But to be your own master, no parents, able to go when and where you wish. To have such freedom, to live...and to love as one wishes," Stephan added in an undertone.

"But you can have the choice of many a fine girl. Could you not find one you could come to love?"

Stephan stuttered uncomfortably. "Yes, yes...I...I...sup...suppose so...but"

"What?" asked Michael gently.

"I...I...don't...know...how...to...say... this."

"We have been close now for a couple of years. You can trust me."

"Well, you are very special to me." he blurted out. "When the sun sets, I hope to see you in my dreams and when the dawn's light graces my window sill, I look forward to the day's arrival so I can see you again. Everything revolves around you!... Now do you understand?!"

Michael was startled but responded kindly.

"This must have been a heavy burden to bear. You were right to tell me because I understand this curse. Every glance must be secret, every sigh must be silent. The yearning goes unrequited. One's very love can cause death to you and your loved one rather than infinite joy.

But you must never speak of this again. There is nothing we can do but suffer in silence. Do you understand?" Michael whispered hurriedly grasping Stephan's hands and looking imploringly into his eyes. "You must understand that the penalty for such a love is death!"

Tears welled up in Stephan's eyes, tears of joy at being accepted and understood and tears of intense sadness that the very source of his joy had to be denied to him. But he understood and nodded yes.

Now that Stephan knew that Michael was like him in his love and desires, he felt even more love for him. It came to a head one afternoon as they were playing a duet outdoors in the orchard. The day was sunny and they took a break to sit down and bask in the warmth.

Michael lay back to look at the clouds and idly chew on a piece of grass. Stephan at first looked at him out of the corner of his eye. The sun glinted gold on his hair and his bright blue eyes sparkled. Stephan felt he must look just like an angel.

"You are so beautiful, you look like an angel, my angel!" blundered Stephan. "My heart is breaking for you. Do you not feel the bond we have? Do I mean nothing to you when you mean the world to me?"

Michael sat up slowly, pondering what to say. He took Stephan's hand in his and, looking into Stephan's eyes, spoke with a choking voice, "Stephan, my dear Stephan, you have no idea how much I am suffering also. Do you not realize how much I love you? I have stayed here for three years now, watching you grow from a boy to a man, feeling closer to you by the day. You are the world to me too, the world, and yet nothing can be done about it."

Tears welled up in Michael's eyes and before Stephan could stop himself, he leaned forward and kissed Michael's hands. As he raised his head, Michael, swept away with love, cradled Stephan's face in his hands and kissed him passionately.

To Stephan, joy beyond measure spread throughout his heart and body. To be loved! And by such a one as Michael! He responded with as much passion as a novice can muster up, marveling at the sensation of his tongue against Michael's. Only then did his loins respond as his heart had. Michael laid him back in the grass and kissed him gently over and over. Stephan's exhilaration knew no bounds.

The silence and beauty of the moment was broken by a thundering shout. "What in God's name are you doing? Have you lost your senses? The devil is here today in our midst and in both of you! Stop at once! You must be purged of this unnatural evil."

Roughly they were yanked apart and onto their feet by the earl's guards. The terror in Michael's eyes spread to Stephan. What had they done?! How could have they been so foolish? How could he live to regret those kisses that a moment earlier had been beyond anything in his life that he had ever experienced?

They were dragged out of the orchard and into the castle, then dragged in different directions, Stephan to his room and Michael to the dungeon. "Michael, where are they taking you? Michael! Michael…"

Michael tried to glance in Stephan's direction but his head was pulled forward by his beautiful curls.

Too frightened to cry, Stephan waited until he was locked in his room before letting out his emotions. He had no idea what was happening to Michael and he paced his room, back and forth, like a caged lion, half crying, half praying. A million thoughts and feelings raced through his mind, each jockeying for position.

After what seemed an hour, the key in his door turned and his father entered the room. His rage was palpable.

"What is the meaning of this!? In God's name, how could you be with another man?!" his father shuddered with disgust. "You, my only son! You must be possessed by the devil! You must be cleansed of the sinful nature!"

He ranted and raved pacing about the room pounding everything that came in contact with him.

"But I love Michael, I have loved him for such a long time, and he loves me, he loves me!" yelled Stephan in surprise.

His father turned to face him and lunged at him. He beat him savagely, pounding his fists into his son who crumpled onto the floor sobbing. His father grabbed him up and raging, with all his strength, flung Stephan against the wall. His head hit the stone and he staggered. But the blow had been too severe. He careened from the wall and fell sharply, his head catching the bed as he collapsed onto the floor. Blood was flowing rapidly from his head and he lost consciousness.

Several days later, when Stephan gained consciousness, he heard his mother's voice:

"Stephan, Stephan, do you hear me?"

He tried to raise his head but excruciating pain met him. Yes, Stephan could hear his mother's voice yet he saw nothing but darkness. Was it night? But no candles were lit for his mother. He blinked his eyelids but still just darkness greeted him.

"Mother, mother, I hear you," he spoke in a cracked broken voice. "But what has happened to my head, why does it hurt so? And why is it so dark? Why do you have no candles? What has happened to Michael? Where is he? I want to see him, please!"

"What do you mean, Stephan. There is no need for candles on this sunny day. Why are you asking for them?" His mother pointedly ignored his reference to Michael.

"No, No, my eyes only see darkness, the darkness of night!" He blinked and blinked but nothing changed. In a panic, he tried to sit up and fell back in agony and into unconsciousness again.

When Stephan came to the second time, the darkness that met him was not as much of a shock as it had been. His mother explained to him that he had severely damaged the back of his head 'in the fall' and no mention was made of his father's part in the incident. Again, he asked, begged his mother about news of Michael but she closed her lips tightly and refused to answer.

One day soon after, his mother came into the room crying. When she came to him, she gently took his hand and stroked his forehead.

"I have something to tell you. I know it will hurt you but you must be strong. Michael was put to the rack, and confessed that you were an unwilling participant in his actions. Charges of rape and sodomy were brought against him and he was executed today. I am so sorry, my dear, so sorry but you will get over it. Grief abates with time."

Little did his mother know. He was now in his thirties and still grieving for a lost love and for a life of love he would never know. Now Genevieve understood his music, the passion of his love and the sorrow of his loss.

But his story wasn't over. For many days, each time he woke, Stephan opened his eyes with the hope of seeing, but it never happened. Slowly he began to realize that he was blind now from the injuries his father had inflicted on him. His father never visited his bedside and when he was well enough to travel, he was sent to the monastery in France, where his father would never have to see or think of him again. It broke his mother's heart but there was nothing she could do. That was how Stephan came to be at Mont Grieff.

Chapter Five

O ne beautiful fall day Genevieve and Evechio decided to walk into town and spend their free day together. After strolling along for half an hour, they came to a stone bridge that marked the entrance to the village. Merchants with their horse and carts clattered over the cobblestones winding their way to the market place to set up their booths. Pots and pans rattled and clanked. Barrels sloshing wine, cider and ale rolled by. A cart with smoked meats was being trailed by a collection of scruffy dogs.

Suddenly the air was filled with a pungent smell. Cheese! Genevieve's mouth watered at the smell and sight of all the cheeses that went by. At the monastery, the cheese was one type only: a hard yellow cheese with a tart flavor. Never the creamy, delicate cheeses that had been her favorites at the chateau. How her life had changed! Here she was in a rough, scratchy robe of a monk, hoofing along in the dust left by carts as they rolled by, grimy and smelly, when she had once ridden on the sleekest of thoroughbreds, dressed in exquisite gowns of velvet and satin, curling her long auburn hair that had flowed down her back.

"Oh, I see you are a lover of cheeses too. You had the look of total rapture on your face as the cart went by. Maybe we can purchase a bite at the market. Where did you pick up a taste for fine cheeses, Jean?

"Where did I learn to love cheeses?' said Genevieve taken off guard. "Um, my father was a close friend of the village cheese vendor and on special occasions, he would give us samples of his cheeses! It was heavenly!"

Genevieve was very aware of her lies and cringed inside that she had to deceive Evechio. One day she promised she would tell him the truth, well, some of the truth. Perhaps the part that she had actually been wealthy at one point, but not that she was a girl. Her very existence depended on her keeping that a secret.

As Evechio promised, they were able to buy a smidgeon of cheese with the few coins his mother had sent him. Genevieve savored every bite much to Evechio's amusement.

After a perusal of the market place, they headed back to the monastery for a quiet evening of prayer.

That summer evening, Father Bernard released the monks from evening prayers. The door of the church had been left open to allow the welcomed summer to come in. The monks were restless and perhaps Father Bernard wanted to enjoy the summer evening as well. He dismissed everyone and the monks filed out one by one. Most of the monks went right back to the monastery to catch up on their sleep but Evechio grabbed Genevieve by the hand and said, "Let's go sit in the orchard and watch the sun set and the evening stars appear."

She was eager to spend some free time with him and readily assented.

Once they were settled on the grass, Genevieve asked him to tell her the story about why his life was dedicated to the church.

"You promised you would tell me one day. I want to know more about you, everything! You are very mysterious to me." Genevieve said teasingly.

"Very well. But first let me tell you that it is a miracle story. Do you believe in miracles?"

"Umm, not really but if you say so, it must be true. I trust you."
Genevieve was eager to hear about a real live miracle. Maybe it
would help her with her wavering faith.

Evechio began his story as Genevieve sat glued to her seat and
watching the light fall upon his face. It struck her as very manly
and she realized he was a man, no longer a boy. His rugged face
and deep brown eyes appealed to her.

EVECHIO'S STORY

"My town is called Castel della Felice, Castle of Happiness, isn't
that a wonderfully romantic name? And the story behind its nam-
ing is very romantic and miraculous. But it was not always known
by that name. In fact, the castle belonged to the very wealthy,
young Count , Dante Bellini, who had a habit of abusing his serfs,
as most 'nobles' do. He was a very handsome man but he had no
wife or children and it was no wonder since he was such a tyrant.
People claimed his heart had been broken, by his brother's wife,
and his sorrow had festered into an acute anger at the world. There
he was amassing more and more wealth with no heirs and he was
not getting any younger. And of course, he drank.

One stormy night he was riding his prized stallion home after
a particularly heavy day of drinking. Now at this same time, a girl
of twelve known as Catarina, was on that same road desperately
looking for her little lost dog. She had gone to bed lonely and
weeping though her parents had tried to comfort her, telling her
that undoubtably the young dog would return by morning. But she
couldn't bear the thought of her little dog out in the dark, lost and
lonely in the storm. Therefore, she had snuck out of the cottage
as soon as she thought her parents were asleep. She had caught
a glimpse of her dog down the road and was running that way to

rescue him. As fate would have it, all three of them converged at the same place at the same time. So there was Catarina, clutching her puppy, frozen in terror with the Count bearing down on them. He had no intention of stopping, but rather thought it would be an exciting feat for his stallion to leap over her. What a strange world we live in that we think animals are stupid and without emotions.

This stallion knew he couldn't make it, what with the slippery, muddy road. The next thing they knew is that the horse swerved to the left and slipped throwing the Count from its back. The Count landed against a rough stone wall of a field. Catarina, cowering on the road, got up when she saw she was safe, and seeing the count lying motionless, she ran to his side.

"Count Bellini, please tell me you are not dead! And all because of me! Please forgive me! Santa Maria, please make him be alive! Will he ever forgive me?" She was weeping.

The Count was not dead, rather his neck had been severely injured. Hearing her words of despair, the Count felt extreme remorse, it is said, and answered that he was alive and it was not her fault, only his own. He tried to raise himself but could not move. Fearing the worst, he told her she must run for help.

"Won't you be afraid all alone in the dark? I wish I could stay to hold your hand! But I will have my dog stay with you while I go. He will stay by your side and protect you at all costs. He is the best dog in the world."

She kissed the Count on the forehead as she had seen her mother do when one of the family was ill, made the sign of the cross and begged Mother Mary to watch over him while she was gone.

As it turned out, Count Bellini was paralyzed from the neck down. Nothing could be done to help him. Because of his wealth, he was set up in his castle with many people to take care of him. But you will see that in many ways, he was saved. His body may have been destroyed but his heart and soul were saved.

In his state of helplessness, he had to depend upon the villagers to tend to him. They were compassionate people and were wonderful with him and in return, his own heart became filled with gratitude and then love for these people. They took turns taking care of him and he in his turn, took care of them with his wealth.

Catarina came to visit him daily out of remorse at first and then out of genuine desire. She entertained him with stories about the village and he taught her to read. Then she would go to his library and choose a book for him and read to him. When Count Bellini had his moments of despair, she was there with her faith to help him see it from a spiritual perspective. They grew to love each other's company and became great confidants and friends.

Not only was he a changed man and a generous man, he had also started a school for the village children, hiring a teacher from Spoleto to move to the castle to set up the school, giving him a large sum of money to buy all the necessary supplies.

The count became the most important person in Catarina's life, her confidant and advisor. Many was the time they discussed the problems of the world and even her petty problems and concerns. Many were the times they shared laughter as well.

Catarina would never forget the time she was fifteen and had had her heart broken. She had fancied a fellow named Emilio and he had claimed to love her too but then she had seen him walking hand in hand with another girl, her best friend no less, then stopping to kiss her. She had run to the castle and trying to conceal her sadness, began to read to the Count. But her voice shook and she had to stop.

"My little Catarina, tonight there is great sadness in you. It is not the sadness of a child, but rather something deeper. But you are hiding it from me. Are you ashamed or do you think I will not understand?"

"My dear Count, I am ashamed. I am crying over a young man! Is that not silly?" she explained in embarrassment.

"That is not silly, there have been a million poems and songs written about this very thing. You are growing up and joining all the others in understanding this sorrow. But you must remember what a beautiful girl you are with your big brown eyes and luxurious long hair, and more important than that, you are a wonderful, loving person. But think about this, my dear. If your lover finds his happiness with another person, you must be happy for him, if you truly loved him to begin with. This is why we are ashamed of love's tears. You are becoming a young lady and will find your love one day. I am certain."

Catarina turned her tear ridden face to the Count's and seeing his compassion and concern, she lay her head on his shoulder, her arms encircling his neck, and cried her heart out, until she felt she could truly understand the count's words.

More than anything, he wanted to raise his withered arms and to stroke her poor sobbing head as it shook on his chest, to caress some comfort into her being. That night he told her the story of his own broken heart, and their bond became complete.

One afternoon, when she was sixteen and had been schooled for several years, she was eager to visit the Count because she had passed her exams. She was scurrying up the circular staircase to his chambers when she heard upraised voices. She stopped immediately, partly out of fear and partly out of respect.

"Have you gone completely insane, Dante?! Your idea is that of a mad man. It is intolerable!"

Catarina recognized the voice of the count's brother who had come for a visit.

"Leave your entire fortune and castle to a bunch of uneducated, lice ridden peasants? Just because they have tended you through a sickness? It's your God given right as an aristocrat to expect such loyalty and devotion from them. They would have been imprisoned for anything less in their behavior! I absolutely forbid it. These lands belong to the family and as your brother, they should come to me after your death!"

He was storming about the room, banging his fists on the furniture in explosions of anger.

"But brother, don't you see? Are you not a Christian? You have more than enough wealth already, plenty for you and your family and your heirs. Why do you need mine? Here we have the opportunity to do an act of unprecedented Christian charity! God brought me this vision, to give all the land and the castle and my money to those who work it! They deserve it. To spread the wealth and education to all men! To eliminate the false distinctions of class. Perhaps others would follow our example and make a paradise of this earth! It is beyond my comprehension that we have been given this power to serve God and man in this way, and have done nothing about it!"

"All I see is that you have been infinitely misguided and deluded by these peons. This idea of yours is demented and no longer worth discussing."

"Very well, since you have no genuine Christian impulse, since I can't appeal to your better nature, listen to this argument. If you were to do as I say, not only would I intercede on your behalf in Heaven when your time came, but your good deed would free you from many years of the torments of purgatory. It might even free you from spending all that money on indulgences that you buy every year from the church. You might enjoy being a better man."

"That argument is baseless. If I wanted to find favor with God and the church, I could simple donate all I inherit from you to the church! That would hold me in good stead for a life time. As it stands in your will, I will receive your holdings as is right. God has seen fit to paralyze you so you can't even change your will if you wanted to. I have nothing more to say to you! Good bye!"

"Please brother, I beg of you! On our mother's grave, do what is right!"

The Count's brother stormed out and flew passed Catarina as she waited outside the room. Catarina raced in to console the count who was in obvious distress and anguish. There he lay, propped up on pillows, his arms limp at his side. Tears streamed down his emaciated face and his frustration was palpable.

"Catarina, God gave me this affliction to lead me to my vision and yet because of this affliction, I can't write to change my will. I had come to see what a blessing this affliction was because it brought me love and grace, compassion and humanity...but now I see that it was perhaps a cruel joke, perhaps the handiwork of the devil, not God!"

Catarina's first impulse was to leave discreetly, embarrassed at witnessing this display of personal grief from the man she had grown to respect and love. But enormous feelings of tenderness filled her soul and she approached him. He was her best friend and companion. A kindred spirit. He had always been a listening ear, a shoulder to cry on, a voice of advice, and a generous protector of her and the other villagers, and now he wanted to give it all to the loyal villagers. Gently she took his hand and placed it against her cheek. Slowly she kissed his hand and began to caress his hair. Moved by his naked sorrow, tears came to her eyes.

"Another broken heart, my dearest Dante?" she whispered smiling. He smiled back, ended his tears, and sighed with resignation.

"You can share this sorrow with me if you want. I have to tell you that I was outside your chamber and heard your brother and you talking. You truly are a saint and perhaps a bit mad, but most saints are, I suppose. You want to leave everything to us. You want to change the world all by yourself."

"You all are ready for this" he responded. "I have been preparing you all for this over the years. The castle is big enough to be turned into your homes, well protected by the ramparts, warm in the winter from the snow and cold. You all will be self-sufficient here with your farms, the forge, the potter, the doctor, the school, and your oldest brother I have trained in the skill of business matters. It will be perfect! The only thing that stands in my way is my will. I have alerted the local judge and priest that I wish a new one, but without my signature, it will not be considered valid. And my brother refuses to honor my wishes."

"Your compassion and generosity know no bounds. What a dreamer and a saint."

"Me a saint, my beloved Catarina? What would have happened to me if I had never met you? Even though it was the vilest of circumstances, I bless the day our paths crossed."

Catarina was so touched by his words that she raised his hand to her lips and kissed it. "When you die, Dante, you will break my heart!"

"Break your heart? How could I?"

"Oh, I know how ashamed you are of your ruined body, but this twisted and lifeless hand is precious to me."

For the first time Catarina realized that she loved Dante, not just loved him as a person, but loved him as a man. Why had she never seen it before? Overcome with emotion, she caught her breath and tears streamed down her face. And that was when the miracle occurred.

Dante felt the tears on his hand as she held it to her, felt her kisses. Was he able to move now? Would he be free of his prison?! Slowly he took his hand and caressed her face. Yes, he could move. Catarina stopped her weeping and looked at him. Was it true? Was he moving? He moved his other arm up and she threw herself into his arms, kissing his face. He took his shaking arms and held her.

"I love you, Dante, I love you!" Catarina cried over and over half weeping and half laughing.

"I think I have always loved you, Catarina. For so many years you have been my light and life, my closest companion. I thought I couldn't love you more but then when you blossomed into a woman, I found I loved you in all ways possible."

Evechio stopped all of a sudden, pretending to clear his throat.

He turned his head away from Genevieve and she realized he was choked up with tears too. "Evechio Dante Bellini, that is my full name...they were my parents...Dante and Catarina.

He claimed it was Catarina's love for him that caused the miracle, that God had looked down on her pure heart and granted him his movement back. He promised God to give him his first-born son as a thank you for His blessing.

He didn't live long after that, the five years he spent paralyzed had taken a toll on his body. No, he did not live long enough to see me born but he managed to change his will and marry my mother in the time he had left."

Genevieve didn't dare move or breathe, sensing the incredible intimacy of this moment, the nakedness of Evechio's heart as he spoke of the miracle of his parents' love. Genevieve worked up the courage to look up into Evechio's face. A single tear was winding its way down his nose. He didn't brush it away, perhaps not wanting to bring attention to the fact he had wept. To Genevieve, that single tear was the most beautiful thing she had ever seen. She wanted to catch it, to hold it, save it as though it were a precious jewel, a diamond. She thought how wonderful that he could be moved as she was and she took his hand, forgetting she was a boy.

Quickly she pulled it back but before she could, he took her hand and squeezed it.

"But there is more. My mother wanted to name the town Castel della Tristezza, Castle of sorrow but the night after I was born, she dreamt of Dante. She dreamt that he was at her side, full and strong, that he picked us up in his arms and took us to the window. The moon was full and bright. We were bathed in its purity and the castle spread out below, silent and peaceful.

He caressed her hair as he had always loved to do and said, "My love, our love made this a place of great love and spirituality, of great compassion and humanity...never before was there such a place...a joyous place...so I ask you, beg you to think of it in this way...call it Castel della Felice, Castle of Happiness so everyone who passes will know of our miraculous love and happiness...many nights since my death, I have walked along the river, watching over the castle...wandering up through the empty streets...and I have come to your room to watch you as you slept, watching as you swelled with child...and I confess I shed a tear, thinking what a perfect family we would have made...but you must let me go, Catarina...you must let joy fill your heart for whatever you feel, I am destined to feel here on the other side...think of the joy you brought me, my little one, throughout my life...I miss you...Think of joy, think of love...think of the happiness...think of... our Castle... of Happiness..."

When she woke from that dream, she wept one last time for my father, wept so hard at the sweetness of his memory, and wept away every last ounce of sorrow she had left. It must have been a painful night for both of them if what my father said was true. But after that she embraced the joys of life again and named the town Castel della Felice, Castle of Happiness."

Evechio shook his head laughing, "And there can't be a town with a truer name! We turned the entire complex into a wonderfully constructed village...the courtyard became one of the best-known market places. The towers and wings of the castle were divided up into homes and more homes were built along the rampart walls. It is truly one of a kind, Jean, you should come the next time I go home.

I forgot to say that in the middle of the courtyard is a statue of a horse and rider bearing down on a little girl holding a puppy. People who come to our village for the first time find it sinister and peculiar, until they hear the story. We who live there smile whenever we see it. So enough!"

Evechio laughed again. "Look at you crying like a girl, we're going to have to toughen you up."

He tousled Genevieve's hair and standing up, gave her his hand to help her up.

"How utterly beautiful! I hope one day I will experience such a love!" she said.

"Jean, you are too young to think of these things!"

Remembering herself as a young boy, she responded "You are right," but in her heart of hearts she knew she was ready for love.

Chapter Six

Genevieve and Evechio had become fast friends. She was like a little brother to Evechio and she, of course, adored his tenderness and loving attention. She was not used to such a sweetness in a man other than Brother Stephan. The fact that he was so handsome was a worry to her lest she develop feelings for him. One particularly hot day, Evechio proposed an outing to Genevieve. He promised she would love it but refused to tell her where they were going.

"Let it be a surprise! You trust me, I hope. You will be thrilled" Evechio said.

After a long, hot walk, they arrived at some woods that were not familiar to Genevieve. Evechio led her through a gnarled collection of laurel shrubs that twisted and turned like tormented beings in hell.

"We should call this the Path of Purgatory. These poor souls are working off their sins in torment!" Genevieve volunteered.

"Jean, you are such an imaginative one! But where this path leads is too pleasant a place to be associated with Purgatory. Wait until you see it. It will be our place alone. No one else would be brave enough to fight through these brambles."

They broke though the undergrowth into the sun shine where she discovered Evechio pointing to a deep, glassy pool of water.

Nestled in the corners here and there were exquisite clusters of waterlilies, looking like porcelain teacups, tinged with pinks and purples and yellows as if placed there by a careless paint brush. On the other side of the pool, grasses covered the banks that stretched out to a small sunny field sprinkled with rosy poppies. It was a paradise! Sunshine and warmth, and cool and refreshing all at once.

"This is too exquisite!"

She turned to agree with and tell Evechio that the laurel path should have no ill-favored names but stammered to a halt. She found that he had completely disrobed and naked, was stretching, eyes closed, arms raised high above his head basking in the sun in pure delight.

"This is glorious! What were you about to say?"

He walked to the edge and with a loud cry of pure joy, dove into the pool, leaving Genevieve stunned and relieved.

His youthful body! She had never seen anything like it. She had found his dark curls, deep brown eyes and strong jaw handsome, but seeing his entire body left her speechless with admiration.

"Well, what are you waiting for, you silly fool! Get in here, it's absolutely spectacular."

She suddenly realized her predicament. He would expect her to disrobe too and then what?

"I better not," she answered searching desperately for an excuse. "Remember that chill I had the other day? I'm not hearty like you."

"Don't be silly, that was nothing. This will strengthen you up, make your blood wake up."

She continued to protest with one feeble excuse after another until, to her utter embarrassment, Evechio teased: "Don't tell me you are ashamed to show your nakedness! Is that the real reason?"

When she lowered her head and blushed, he hooted with laughter.

"Very well, I'll turn my back and close my eyes," he volunteered when he saw her continued distress.

"Promise on the Holy Bible?"

"Yes, I promise, but why should it matter if I see your naked-ness? You can't possibly think I'm interested in young boys! Especially after all the times I've held you through the night and nothing happened."

There was a slight tone of anger in his voice and Genevieve felt he had every right to be angered by her distrust. It grieved her to pretend to distrust him after he had proven himself a total gentle-man over and over, but unfortunately it was critical to her survival.

"Thank you," she offered up meekly. "I'm sorry. I've always been shy this way. I'm small and pale and scarred, not a pretty sight to behold."

Once he had turned away, she quickly fumbled out of her robe and her undergarment. Trembling, she unwound the cloth she used to bind her small breasts. Slowly she lowered herself into the dark green waters, grateful that it would conceal her body from him.

"I'm in. You can turn around now."

She did not feel very adventurous being inhibited as she was but she still was able to enjoy the caress of the waters against her bare flesh. On the other hand, Evechio was like a school boy, splash-ing her, diving and surfacing like a dolphin, wanting to wrestle with her. She had to protest, though every inch of her loved his playfulness.

Finally, she retreated to the grassy bank, clothing herself as quickly as possible. Then she sat on the bank watching him. Suddenly she felt old, defeated by her life and misfortunes, so envious of his carefree ways. Today I am the guardian and he is the child, she thought, and waves of tenderness flooded her as she watched him wistfully. Lost in reverie, she was startled when he scrambled out of the water and threw himself on the ground beside her.

"The sun shall dry me!" he laughed as he rolled onto his back and arched his arms behind his head.

The prospect of feigning comfort with his naked body made Genevieve lose her breath. Quickly she looked away to compose herself.

"So what do you think? Not a bad specimen, wasted as a monk."

"What…what are you saying?" she asked pretending to be elsewhere occupied.

"This, me, my body. Girls told me it was a waste that I was going to be a monk. What do you think?"

To her horror, she realized he was expecting an opinion from her on the glories of his body. She simply would have to look at him now. How could he ask her such a thing? The arrogance! Maybe he was just being brotherly, or trying to make her less self-conscious, that bodies should be considered natural and beautiful. Perhaps he hoped she would feel comfortable enough to ask him some question about her own "boy's" body that might have been troubling her.

"Yes, very good," she answered brusquely after a quick look.

She casually rolled over on her stomach so she could no longer be confronted by his indeed exquisite form.

"Well, I can tell you are not impressed."

He turned his face to the sky and began to reminisce about his boyhood in Italy. She listened in fascination as he talked about his mother, his cousins and so many people in the village he loved: always someone to play with, or a shoulder to cry on. It seemed to have been an idyllic childhood.

After that day, Genevieve was noticing a heightened awareness of Evechio's presence. She was on constant alert and felt her heart jump whenever he appeared. Sitting next to him at meals, she was keenly aware of the warmth and closeness of his body. One day, she glanced at him during supper and noticed his wrist protruding from his robe, his hand gently resting on the table next to her. She was fascinated by the strength of his wrist, the softness of the dark hair that started there. His fingers were sturdy and clean, not tapered and feminine like Stephan's. She was suddenly overwhelmed with the thought of Evechio's hands caressing her hair, her face. She felt faint from the power of the emotion, the strength of the desire and the shock of having these feelings for him. He had been like a brother to her and knew her only as a boy.

Suddenly embarrassed that someone might guess her thoughts, she blushed and took a deep breath. Secretly she glanced around but all the monks were busy with their bowls of soup and chunks of bread, silently eating as was their way.

When the bell rang to indicate that the meal was over and the prayers were chanted, Genevieve stumbled clumsily off the bench. Evechio reached to help her but she hastily pushed him away. In single file they exited from the dining hall and walked in line to the chapel for evening service, prayers and meditation. Genevieve was secretly delighted to be able to stare at Evechio's back as he walked before her. But once again, she blushed with the guilt of such emotions. As well, she realized how hopeless the situation was, she could never reveal herself to him or realize the fantasy of his caress. She forced herself to look down to the floor instead of at his back.

That evening, the service crept slowly along. Genevieve just wanted to be alone with her thoughts and away from Evechio. During prayers, she prayed for her feelings to go away, for it to just be a passing fancy. But then during the long hours of meditation, all she could think about was Evechio. What was wrong with her? She couldn't continue with these thoughts. It would ruin everything. How could she continue to be his close friend under the circumstances? She felt she would die inside every time he touched her from now on.

At last, the evening was over and the monks were dismissed from chapel to retire to their cells. Genevieve wove her way impatiently through the group of monks and rushed through the dark up to her chamber and quickly jumped into bed. She knew she couldn't face Evechio.

Soon she heard him in the next room and then her door opened. He held his candle and approached her pallet. He knelt holding the candle high so he could see her face. She desperately pretended to sleep. Then she felt his hand brush her hair away from her forehead.

"Sweet Dreams, Jean" he whispered and left.

Genevieve was electrified, wide awake now. How could she sleep? She kept reliving his caress on her forehead and touched the spot lovingly. Oh, what would she do, what could she do? Nothing!

As the days went on, Genevieve's feeling did not abate. As a result, she avoided Evechio as much as possible and behaved awkwardly in his presence. She was thankful that he didn't seem to notice.

The next time Genevieve had a chance to see Stephan, she raced to the orchard to talk with him. Maybe he could help her.

"Stephan, hello" she greeted him as she reached his favorite spot. "I need to talk with you. Perhaps you can help me!"

"Help you? Help you with what, Jean?"

"You have shared so many secrets with me. But now I have one and there is nobody else here I can talk to about this."

"What about?"

"What has happened is that I am having such strong feelings and they are disrupting my life here at the monastery. I can't stop thinking about being touched by and touching somebody. It's so overpowering!"

"Oh, those feelings. They are perfectly normal for someone your age. So you have been imaging girls?"

Genevieve paused before answering. Should she confess the truth to Stephan? Should she keep pretending she was a boy and thinking now about girls or should she tell him the truth?

"Well? Am I correct? No need to be embarrassed," Stephan reassured her. "Yes, it's that kind of thoughts," she said evasively.

"Jean, you will go through a period of having those thoughts especially at this age. You haven't committed yourself to a life as a monk yet. Perhaps it's not for you. If those feelings really continue to bother you, perhaps you could find a girl in the village to court. See if that is what you really want. You know that I wanted to follow the path of love. But now peaceful contemplation is what I need. I don't have those thoughts anymore."

Genevieve twirled a piece of grass, too embarrassed to look Stephan in the face but grateful for his words.

"Thank you, Stephan. I think I understand. I have to live with this for a while and hope it goes away. I don't think I'll be doing any courting."

"Very well. I pray it goes easily with you."

Chapter Seven

S oon after Genevieve's conversation with Stephan, sickness came to the monastery. Its cause was unknown but soon several of the monks were taken over by an intense fever. Delirium set in and the monks needed to be tended to at all times. Genevieve was not called to help as she was considered too young for such an important job but when Stephan fell ill, she begged to be his attendant. Her love for him was strong and she didn't trust anyone else to care for him as she would.

Stephan was already in the stages of delirium when she was given permission to attend to him. She knew she had to try to keep him cool and hydrated. She continually mopped his brow and chest with cool well water and sat him up periodically to get him to drink. In his delirium, he talked about his youth and his dead lover, reliving conversations they had had. Sometimes he smiled and laughed and other times he cried out and wept. Genevieve tried to comfort him at those times but it has hard to reach him in his delirium.

She stayed with Stephan, day and night. This offered her an escape from seeing Evechio, which was a relief. But soon the days wore on and she found herself exhausted. She lay on the palette next to Stephan and slept whenever she could. It was fitful sleep because she was always aware of Stephan and his needs and disturbed by his mutterings and rantings.

The time came when Genevieve became feverish herself. When Brother Michael came to give her supper, he saw her feverish condition and called for help. He picked her up and carried her to her chamber. He summoned Evechio from the dining hall with the news that Jean was now ill and in need of care. Evechio rushed to Genevieve's side, frantic with worry. He bathed her face with cold water and began to loosen her robe to bathe her chest. In spite of her raging fever, Genevieve knew she couldn't let Evechio open or remove her robe. She struggled to push his hands away.

"No! No! Leave me alone. Don't touch me. Please, please, just leave me" she ranted.

"Jean, it's the fever talking. I know you are bashful but you must get the right treatment. This fever is dangerous. I must cool you down."

"NO! I'm fine this way. Just wash my face and give me water to drink," she replied angrily.

Not wanting to fight her, Evechio agreed to do as she asked. But as the night went on, she fell into a delirium and was no longer cognizant of her surroundings and Evechio.

Now Evechio felt he could disobey her orders and disrobe her. As he pulled the robe up over her body, he gasped in utter shock. Her secret was revealed.

Evechio was completely shaken by his discovery. All the times he had lain next to Jean, held her during her miserable moments, swam naked in front of her, every touch flashed before his face. He blushed with intense embarrassment. Then he found himself trembling with shock, not knowing what to think or to do. Jean was a girl, no, a young woman. She had been disguising herself all this time! Did the abbot know? Why was she doing this? What or who was she hiding from? Could he, should he keep her secret? What would happen to her if he told? Would she be sent away in disgrace? A myriad of questions flooded his mind. His head began to throb. He knew he would have to make a decision and live with the consequences of it.

Evechio lowered her robe and continued to bathe her head with cold water, praying for guidance and for her recovery. When he propped her up to drink, he was keenly aware of her femaleness and held her gently. Waves of tenderness flooded him as he mopped her brow and watched her as she lay there so helplessly. Jean, a girl! He just couldn't believe it. He thought and thought and finally came to a decision. He would tell no one. He couldn't betray her. There must be good reason for her to be here. She must be hiding from something terrible. No, he couldn't betray her. He cared for her too much.

In her delirium, Genevieve muttered and ranted. She called out Delphine's name and wept. She thrashed wildly yelling "No! Robert, no!" When Evechio tried to calm her, she yelled, pushing him away "No Robert, don't touch me, please!" and finally whimpering, she turned on her side to face the wall.

As the night progressed, so did her fever. Evechio became desperate, trying to cool her down. Nothing seemed to be working and he finally decided he must remove her heavy robe, to bathe her entire body in cool water. He was certain that her secret would be safe from the other monks since none of them ever ventured up into the tower. He slowly pulled her robe from around her and came to the wrappings that she used to bind her breasts. So that's how she did it, he thought. He removed the wrappings and gently rolled her onto her stomach to allow her more privacy.

As he went to wipe down her back, he became aware of uneven stops. Curiously, he raised his candle to see and was stunned to see a series of welts, scars on her back. Someone had whipped her and so harshly, it had done permanent damage. Evechio fought back tears and traced the scars ever so gently with his fingers. It was clear to him that Jean, or whatever her name was, had many painful secrets. Well, he was glad she was safe now and he knew for sure he would never betray her. He would do whatever was in his power to protect her.

The next day was awkward for Evechio. He was still in shock and uncertain what to do. Should he tell her that he knew the truth? Now everything between them would be strained and different. What excuse could he use if she asked him to sleep with her on cold nights as they were in the habit of doing? Though he was relieved that she was better, he wished he had more time to think it through.

His thoughts were interrupted by the sound of Genevieve stirring.

"Evechio" she managed to say in a strained voice. "Evechio, am I well again? How is Brother Stephan?"

He looked down on her lying on her palette. She looked so pale and fragile and he wondered that he had never realized she was a girl. He saw it now, the beautiful delicacy of her face, the rich auburn hair, and softness of her voice. She reached out her arm for him and he knelt beside her.

"Your fever has broken and you will be fine...Jean," he added the name hesitantly. "Brother Stephan is still struggling but is being cared for."

She took his hand in hers and brought it to her lips for a kiss. He quickly pulled his hand away. Puzzled she said:

"Thank you, Evechio, I can't think of anyone I would rather to have looked after me."

"Go back to sleep...Jean. I will bring you food later to restore your strength."

She gave him one last look, shut her eyes and settled back to sleep.

That afternoon Evechio brought Genevieve some oatmeal just as she liked it, with lots of raisins and honey. He helped her sit up and she managed to eat all her food though slowly.

As the days went on, Genevieve gathered up her strength and was soon ready to return to her duties. Brother Stephan continued to be weak and unable to work. He was given permission to stay in his cell, with the hope that he would recover. Genevieve worried about him every day.

The day came when Father Bernard called her into his chambers. She wondered what she had done to deserve his attention. Had she done something wrong? Reluctantly she entered, knelt and kissed his hand.

"Rise, Jean, I just wanted to tell you that Brother Stephan has been asking for you. He is very weak and his breathing is labored. I fear the worst. Can you go to him as soon as possible?"

Genevieve's heart sank and tears formed in her eyes. Brother Stephan was still that ill? That was a terrible sign. She must speak to him and see for herself how he was doing.

"Yes, Father, I will go immediately"

Genevieve raced up the stairs to the monk's quarters. One of the brothers was in Stephan's room tending to him. He politely left when Genevieve arrived.

Stephan, already thin, was even thinner. His pale face was drawn with pain and his breathing has irregular. He held is hand out to Genevieve and it was cold and clammy. She took it with both her hands and rubbed it to warm it.

"Jean, I wanted to…thank you…. for being my friend…." he said pausing between words to catch his breath. "I am so glad …I told you my…secret. If I die…I will feel better… knowing that my story…has been told…and will live on in your memory."

Overcome by worry, Genevieve kissed his hand and gathered her composure before she responded.

"Dearest Stephan, I too am glad to be the carrier of your story. I will never forget you and the love you once had. Please know that it will live on in me!"

Then she could contain herself no longer and burst into tears.

"Don't upset yourself, Jean… I am happy to go… if it is my time… Now leave so I might rest."

Genevieve gave his hand one last kiss and left weeping.

Genevieve was so upset that she knew she needed to speak to Evechio. She raced to his room where he was getting ready for his work in the scriptorium. She threw herself into his arms weeping.

"Evechio, I'm afraid Brother Stephan is dying! I can't bear it. He has had such a pained life. It's not fair! How could God do this?"

Evechio hesitated and then put his arms around her and stroked her hair. What should he do? he thought. This was no longer correct behavior now that he knew she was a girl. Slowly he pushed her away from him and looked away. He couldn't bear to see her tear-stained face.

"He will be fine, Jean, he just needs the spring to come and warm his body and his soul. Don't worry. Now I must go or I'll be late."

He turned and left the room. Startled by his brusque behavior, Genevieve felt even worse than before. She went to her room and sobbed into her pillow until exhausted, a serenity came to her. She pulled herself together and went to her work practice in the kitchen. Embarrassed because her eyes were red from crying, she looked at no one and chopped her vegetables in silence.

Chapter Eight

Genevieve noticed a change in Evechio. He seemed distant and even seemed to avoid her. He would not make eye contact with her and rushed to get ready in the mornings so she had no time to talk to him. She felt a huge void in her life. Evechio, for his part, was having a hard time looking at Genevieve. Now that he knew she was a girl, he was struck by her beauty. Even in the robes, he was aware of her body. He already felt great tenderness for her as Jean. Now he was struggling with his emotions every day.

A few days later, the temperature dropped. Snow had fallen in the night. As Genevieve finished her day, she realized how freezing she was. Her room was so cold and she knew that on these nights, Evechio would come to sleep with her to keep her warm. She clambered under the covers and called to him in the next room.

"Evechio, come here. I'm freezing! I need your warmth." Evechio peered into her room but didn't enter.

"I think I need to sleep in my room tonight. You will warm up soon under the blankets."

He closed the door without even saying good night or sweet dreams. Confused by his distance, Genevieve felt hurt. Why was he behaving this way, distant and unaffectionate? Why had he changed towards her?

Later in the night, Genevieve woke shivering. Her teeth were chattering and she felt she couldn't bear it. Should she go to Evechio's room and climb in his bed? She pulled herself out of her bed and scampered over to the door, opened it carefully and slowly crawled under his covers.

She nestled herself against him to gather his warmth. But before she could warm herself, she felt Evechio moving away from her. The next thing she knew, he was pushing her out of his bed.

"You can't do this, we can't do this, it's not right! You must leave!"

"But I don't understand, we have always kept each other warm on the cold nights. You have changed and I don't understand why? What have I done to displease you so?!"

Genevieve started to cry thinking she had lost her friendship with Evechio.

Evechio suddenly felt terribly guilty. She had no idea why he was behaving in this manner. She was innocent of his knowledge. Couldn't they go on as before?

Tenderly, he took her in his arms and held her. She stopped her weeping and nestled into his embrace.

"Can I stay then?" she asked timidly.

"Yes, dear Jean, you can stay."

He kissed her on the forehead and they settled down to sleep.

As the cold nights went on, innocently, she snuggled next to him, unaware of his struggles. He did everything to contain himself but each night it was more difficult. His tenderness and fondness for Jean had become stronger now that he knew she was a girl. Her beauty haunted him during the day as he worked in the scriptorium and interrupted his prayers. He found himself eagerly anticipating their moments together and felt extremely self-conscious as he walked in front of her in line. He wondered what she was thinking about him. He wondered what she was doing hiding here in the monastery. Did Father Bernard know? His nights were restless, full of confusing dreams about her.

One particularly cold night, the two of them were snuggled in bed. They fell asleep as usual, spooning. Genevieve awoke with a start when she felt Evechio's hardness pressed against her. Her heart sank. Was he like Stephan, interested in boys? Was she just a sexual being to him? She had been fighting her feelings for him for the longest time and now she was to be disappointed by his sexual preference. And young boys at that!

She pulled away from him and turned to face him. They had left the candle burning to give them the illusion of warmth so she could see his face full of lust.

"How could you?! How could you do this to me? Are you no better than…." She realized she couldn't say Robert or her husband without betraying herself.

Evechio reached his hand behind her head and drew her near. He kissed her tenderly. In spite of her thoughts, she melted at his touch.

After the kiss, she looked down in shame.

"I know" was all he said. "I know. And I love you, whom ever you are. You are dearer to me than my family."

"You know?! How long have you known? I was unaware of your knowledge! And it was so hard for me to lie to you after our closeness. It was torture to be so close to you, to love you and know I couldn't act on it. But you know!"

He turned her head up again and kissed her passionately, their bodies pressed together. They kissed for a while longer, exploring each other's lips and then Evechio stopped. "We need to talk! Who are you? What are you doing here? Why are you pretending to be a boy? I have so many questions to ask you?"

"First you must tell me how you found out!" Genevieve asked.

"It was when you were so sick. I tended to you and you had such a high fever, I had to take off your robe and chemise. I found the binding you use to hide your breasts. I had to remove everything and cool you down with a wet cloth. I even saw your back with its scars. It saddened me so!"

"So that's why you were so different! It pained me so to see the change in you. But I will tell you my story. No more lies!"

"First tell me your name? I will treasure it!" he answered.
"Genevieve, I am Genevieve"

"Genevieve, what a beautiful name, Genevieve! Now tell me everything."

Genevieve took a deep breath and began her story. They talked all night as she described her childhood, her marriage, the death of Delphine. What she couldn't bear to tell him was the sexual degradation she had experienced at her husband's hands. She was too shy and embarrassed. Finally, she came to her escape and her need to hide as a boy, far from her husband.

Evechio held her closely during the painful parts of her story, stroking her hair. "So how old are you?"

"I am actually fifteen years old now. Fortunately, I am small and have small breasts so I can pass as a young boy, but that won't last for long. They will wonder why my voice hasn't changed soon enough."

The next thing they knew was the sound of the morning bell. They had talked the entire night. Reluctantly they gave each other one finally embrace and rose to face the new day.

Chapter Nine

Now that they had professed their love for each other, they couldn't wait for the moments in the day when they were together. They spent every night nestled together, whispering to all hours, getting to know each other better.

One hot summer night, they removed their robes and climbed into bed in their chemises. As Evechio turned away to give her privacy, Genevieve removed the wrappings around her breasts. Suddenly aware of herself as a girl becoming a woman, she felt aroused and took off her chemise completely. When she turned back to Evechio, she was completely naked and excited by the intimacy.

"Evechio, you can turn around now, my love!"

When he turned, he saw her nakedness in the candle light. It took his breath away.

Genevieve said: "Your turn now! I want to see you naked again and know you are mine this time!"

He suddenly thought back to the day of their swim and how he had lain naked next to her. He blushed but eagerly removed his chemise. The dark hair on his chest glistened in the candlelight and Genevieve caressed his chest. Not sure what she should do next, she lay down on the bed to await his touch. He rolled over on his side next to her and wove his hand along her face, down her throat till he reached her breasts. He moved in and kissed her throat and moved his head down to her breasts. He cupped one in his hand and kissed the nipple gently. Genevieve had never experienced such gentle seduction. Then before she could stop him, he had moved his hand down between her legs. He was caressing her between her thighs and was moving upward. She felt an electricity shoot through her at his touch. Ever so slowly, he moved his hand as far up as he could and rubbed gently. Genevieve gasped in pleasure, shocked that love making could feel so good. Instinctively she spread her legs and Evechio climbed on top of her. Propping himself up with both arms, he gazed into her face as he entered her. She was beyond thought she was so full of pleasure. His steady rocking in and out, up and down drove her to ecstasy and she felt herself open and surrender fully to his passion. Unable to contain herself, she cried out in pleasure and Evechio moaned in response, giving one final thrust before collapsing. Their mouths found each other in a passionate kiss and he rolled off next to her. They held each other closely, kissing and caressing each other gently.

"I love you, every inch of you drives me wild!" he confessed. "I think of you all the time and can barely contain myself when we sit next to each other in church and at meals."

"Me too. I have to walk behind you in line and want to grab you right there. I picture you naked under your robes! It is unbearable. I live for the moments I see you and the nights we spend together."

Having discovered the pleasures of love-making, Genevieve couldn't get enough. Her playful side came out after she gained confidence in her nakedness and his passion for her. But she still could not tell him about her experiences with Robert.

Evechio and Genevieve cherished their private time together. Pretending to be a young boy had become harder and harder for her as her love for Evechio grew. But they had to continue their pretense at all costs.

Chapter Ten

O ne free afternoon, they decided to walk into the town, to treat themselves to something to eat, monastery food being so basic. Once they arrived, Evechio suggested they visit a different part of town.

"Let's go in the back streets to see how the other half lives. It's important that we don't forget how lucky we are."

Evechio turned down a narrow dirt road where half-timbered houses stood one against the next. Villagers sat on benches outside their small houses or stood in doorways chatting with their neighbors. Genevieve was suddenly aware of two young women with painted faces and whose skirts were pinned up on one side to reveal their petticoats and stockinged legs. Their bodices were loosely laced and falling off a shoulder, revealing the start of an ample bosom.

Their reddened lips pursed into a kiss as Evechio approached and they called out, laughing: "Father, father, I fear I have sinned, would you hear my private confession?" while they cocked their heads to one side flirtatiously.

"It's a sin to make a man of the cloth so handsome!" added the other woman. Evechio laughed and winked at them good naturally and responded:

"I'll think of you in my prayers tonight, my good ladies!"

The women giggled, clearly flattered by his joke and bowed as Genevieve and Evechio passed by.

"Why wait until tonight to pray when your prayers can be answered right now!" they called after him.

Addressing Genevieve, they called:

"And what about you, boy, I'm sure you've never been with a woman and have no idea what you are giving up. Let us initiate you to the pleasures of the secular world!"

By this time, Genevieve was blushing profusely, shocked as well that Evechio would flirt with this kind of woman. She was also suddenly aware of her drab, unfeminine appearance.

Pushed passed her breaking point, she yelled back at them:

"Never, you women are the scum of the earth, you filthy whores!" Evechio's face tightened in anger.

"How dare you judge these women! You have no idea who they are or what circumstances led them to this life. Poverty is an ugly master and we all have our price, remember that, we all have our price!"

Genevieve was shocked by his anger and her own. Her attitude and hatred were the result of her days with her husband and the constant parade of prostitutes he brought back to their home. He wanted them to instruct her in the ways to please him and it turned her stomach. She often wondered how the members of her own sex could betray her, humiliate her.

She was shattered by Evechio's response. What was he really saying? The man she trusted more than anyone in the world was rebuking her for these feelings, how could he! Suddenly it was more than she could bear. Was he betraying her too? Saying her husband had the right to humiliate her so and had the right to expose her to the company of these women? How could Evechio!? Was this world such a place that there was no one she could trust? How could I have been such a fool to trust him, love him?

"I hate them, I hate them! I hate you, too!" she cried, bursting into tears. She felt his strong grip on her wrists holding down the fists she had formed to fight him. She struggled wildly, weeping as he excused themselves and dragged her off to privately comfort her.

"How could you? How could you? I trusted you. I trusted you and you're just like him, just like him!" she added hysterically.

"My little one, what are you talking about?! Why are you so upset? I hate seeing you this way. I would never do anything to hurt you. You've become closer to me and more important to me than anyone. Where are these accusations coming from?"

Evechio's concern and distress with her sorrow calmed her of her hysteria. He sensed her submission and gently wrapped her in his strong arms, cradling her distraught face against his chest with one hand.

"Genevieve, where do your anguishes come from, your nightmares, your sorrow?! Why do I sense there is so much more than you are telling me? How can I avoid hurting you and help heal your frail spirit if I don't know all the truth? God, I want more than anything to heal you! To make my love be everything you need, to make my arms at night keep away your tears, my smile during the day keep away your sorrows. I love you! I need to protect you to feel complete. You make me hate Robert for what affect he's had on you. How could anyone have ever willingly harmed my precious Genevieve? How could they?"

Genevieve turned her tear-stained face to Evechio with such an utter expression of gratitude, like a little dog lonely and abandoned finally finding a home and loving master. To her amazement, tears had collected in Evechio's deep eyes as he looked with overwhelming tenderness at her.

"God, now do you see how much I love you? How much I care for your happiness? Your safety? Your joy? Every inch of you is dear to me, from your beautiful curls to your tiniest toe! Your tender breasts to your pale pink lips! From your sorrowful green eyes that always keep me guessing about your pain to the angelic dirty, tear-stained face!"

So overcome with emotion, he clinched her tightly against him, half crying, half laughing as he groaned, "God, I love you, don't ever leave me, do you hear?! I beg of you, don't ever leave me!"

He held her away from him so he could take a good look at her.

"My God, Genevieve, how did you ever do this, how did you ever get me to forget my vows to God and my vows to myself! What a rascal you are, what a rascal! And I couldn't be happier!"

Evechio's overt affection and declaration of love had left Genevieve exquisitely happy and speechless. She blushed under his gaze and looked hastily down at the dusty road beneath her feet. This man was more than she could possibly have dreamed of: young and strong, tender and loving, affectionate and fun, a man of the world and a man of God. How could he totally change her mood from despair and rage to such utter joy? Of course, she trusted him, how could she have had any doubts, but it still troubled her that any human being could have that much effect on her. Hadn't she sworn that she would never trust anyone except herself, that she would never involve anyone in her troubles, never risk anyone else's life but her own?

"My dear, I've left you speechless, have I?"

Evechio smiled down at her, putting his arm around her shoulder and they continued on their way once again posing as a monk and his favorite novice on a day on the town.

Now that Genevieve and Evechio were lovers, they sought to spend time away from the monastery as much as possible. One of their favorite places to go was the secluded swimming hole. On a hot summer day, they made their way through the tangle of branches and brush to the pond. This time Genevieve wasted no time stripping down, reveling in her nakedness. And this time, she didn't avoid looking at Evechio's nakedness. She was particularly drawn to his hips and how they led down to his thighs. She found it very alluring.

Evechio scrambled out of his clothes and jumped right in. Genevieve was a bit more tentative and was enjoying the feel of the sun's warmth on her skin. She stretched in the sunlight.

"Come on in, you temptress! What are you trying to do? Drive me wild with the sight of your beautiful body!" Evechio teased.

"No, I'm just worshipping the sun! It feels so good on my flesh!" she replied. "But I will come in to keep you company."

Genevieve entered the water and swam slowly up to Evechio. He opened his arms and she nestled into his embrace. The sensuality of the water touching every inch of her flesh enhanced her excitement. Here she was in the arms of her lover. She pressed her body against his and kissed him deeply. He responded with growing excitement and she relished the knowledge that he wanted her. Wrapping her legs around him, she allowed him to enter her. She was in heaven.

After their mutual delight and satisfaction, they played in the water like two little children, splashing and laughing, diving deep and bursting up to the surface.

As they lay on the banks to dry in the sun's light, Genevieve had a hard time keeping her hands to herself and she rolled over and pressed herself against Evechio, tracing her fingers along his chest on down to his belly where she rested her hand. He grabbed her hand and placed it on his member. His arousal excited her. He pulled her on top of him and they made-love again. The seclusion of the place left her feeling very uninhibited and she moaned loudly. She loved the moment when Evechio fully surrendered to their love-making and his moans of pleasure were followed by a deep sigh.

They lay in each others' arms for the longest time and soon the sun lowered itself on the horizon.

"It must be late afternoon, my love, we best be going," Evechio said.

"Yes, my dear, we should get dressed and hurry back. It will be dinner soon and we don't want anyone wondering where we are."

Genevieve solemnly gathered up her chemise and robe, tied back her hair and dressed reluctantly. Pretending she was a boy had become such a challenge for her. She wanted to shout out to the world how much she now loved being a woman and how much she loved Evechio.

How much longer could she go on denying herself and pretending? She was sure they would betray their passion for each other, that someone would notice it. Then all hell would break loose. What were they to do? She asked Evechio his thoughts on the matter.

"Sweetheart, I am so worried that someone will find out about us and about me. It would be devastating for the community. What would the monks think, knowing they had been living with a woman. They would feel so betrayed and compromised. We must do something and soon. We can't go on like this. I know it has only been a couple of months but we should make a decision. I feel I should leave but where would I go?" she added sadly.

Evechio dropped everything and turned towards her.

"What are you talking about!? Leaving?! Never, I couldn't bear it! It's true that we can't go on as we are."

Genevieve's heart sank. Not to go on as they were? Did he mean they would have to give each other up? How could she bear it. Did she mean so little to him that he could easily relinquish her? Tears formed in her eyes and she turned away from him.

"Alright, we can stop this right now if you wish, if you think it is for the best." she said hiding her emotion.

"Is that what you want? I will do whatever you wish," he said hiding his own emotions.

"It sounds like that is what you wish, to be done with me!" she replied unable to hide her bitterness.

"My God, do you really think I could live without you? I am so deeply in love with you! Every angle of your face and curve of your body drives me wild. But more than that, you are dearer to me than the world. I couldn't go on without you! These have been the happiest months of my life. I don't want them to end."

He grabbed her hand and she turned towards him. He saw the tears in her eyes and kissed them away. He held her close in his deep embrace and she knew she was home. This was where she belonged at any cost.

"So what should we do?"

"We obviously must leave the monastery and go out into the world where we can unabashedly be together. I can find work and we can live together! I know we can't marry but I don't mind. I would live with you under any conditions, as your slave if needed! I love you, Genevieve, and nothing will change that!"

Genevieve's heart soared at his words, go away together, live together. She couldn't imagine wanting anything more from life. Now they would have to make plans.

"My dearest love, I am so happy I can't tell you. I love you beyond all limits. Where shall we go? How can we pay to get there? We are penniless!"

"You forget I come from a rich family. I will contact my mother and tell her all about you and our plans. I pray she will understand and send us some money. I will write her immediately. When I have heard from her, we will talk to Father Bernard and tell him the truth. We owe him that."

"Evechio, I am the happiest girl in the world! We will be together as man and wife, to love each other purely and fully, unashamedly."

With excitement at the prospect, they kissed deeply and then hurried home to the monastery.

Chapter Eleven

As the days passed, Evechio and Genevieve grew more and more restless. Evechio had written to his mother to tell her of his deep love for Genevieve, and that he could not continue as he was to become a monk. He hoped she would understand and forgive him.

Soon after he received a letter from her. With trepidation. he opened it.

"My Dear Evechio,

Who am I to judge you and the depth of your love for Genevieve? I would be a hypocrite to discount these feelings as I was blessed with a profound love myself. Perhaps it was selfish of Dante and of me to commit you to a life as a monk. We should have thought of another way to honor God. Since it is clear you must leave the monastery, I would suggest you go to Florence to start your new life. There is much work there and it is a city full of joy. It will be an exciting place to start your life together.

I embrace you,
Mother"

Evechio was ecstatic with his mother's acceptance of his love and rushed to tell Genevieve.

"Now we must tell Father Bernard. This will be so hard as he has been so good to me," Genevieve responded. "I feel so ashamed that I tricked him and the other monks and have taken away one of his promised monks."

Late that evening, they requested an audience with Father Bernard. Standing before his desk, Genevieve was suddenly filled with shame and could only look down at the floor. But sensing Evechio's presence next to her gave her courage. She raised her eyes.

"Good evening, Brother Evechio and Jean, what is so important that you both need to speak to me in private?"

"Father, we need to beg your forgiveness. We have been deceiving you!"

"Deceiving me? How is that?"

Genevieve knew she should be the one to tell him the truth. She put her hand on Evechio's arm, and looked at him.

"I think I must be the one to tell Father Bernard my truth."

Turning to Father Bernard, she lowered her eyes again in embarrassment.

"Father, I have come to Mont Grieff under false pretenses. Yes, it is true I had to leave a place of great brutality for my own safety and that Pere LeMaitre chose Mont Grieff, knowing my truth. He is a man of great compassion. But I am not who I seem. I am actually Genevieve, a girl of fifteen, and it was not an abusive father I left, but a husband. I have been hiding here from him."

She glanced up to see how Father Bernard had taken the news.

"My Lord, what have I allowed here at Mont Grieff?! A girl living with monks! I am shocked and appalled. I need a moment to take this in!"

He closed his eyes and clasped his hands together in prayer. Evechio and Genevieve waited silently until Evechio finally spoke up.

"Father, that is not all we have come to say. Genevieve and I have become very close, so close that we are in love. I am planning on leaving Mont Grieff with her now that she must go. We will be going to Florence. When would you like us to leave?"

"What! Both of you are leaving? I am losing two novices? And the vows of chastity have been broken here at Mont Grieff?! How could you do this to me and God and your vows?!"

"Can you ever forgive us?" Genevieve pleaded.

"I need time to understand and accept this in order to forgive you. This is a profound transgression! Under the circumstances you must leave immediately and never tell anyone about Jean... Genevieve. You will leave this very night!"

Father Bernard stood and turned his back to them. They had been dismissed.

A carriage was summoned for them. Genevieve went to bid farewell to Chestnut who had become a monastery horse. She knew she could not bring him with her and that he would continue to be well cared for at the monastery.

"My dear Chestnut, you saved my life when I fled from Robert. You helped me start a new life where I have found happiness at last. You have been a faithful servant and a treasured friend. I will never forget you!"

Weeping, she embraced him and he nuzzled her. She reluctantly turned and left, glancing over her shoulder one last time.

Then she moved on to the graveyard. Stephen had been buried there that winter and she had been placing flowers on his grave. She knew this was the last time she could do so and she broke down weeping. Tenderly she traced his name on the grave stone and whispered a prayer for his soul. Distraught, she rushed back to Evechio's embrace.

Evechio and Genevieve were not allowed to say good-bye to any of the monks and fortunately the monks were in bed. The moon's light enveloped them as they headed off to their new life. Holding hands in the carriage, they felt a huge excitement about the future. They would be allowed to openly express their love for one another, no more hiding, no more shame. It felt good to be alive.

PART FOUR:
Florence

Chapter One

Genevieve was living happily with Evechio in Florence. They had found a room to live in with its own private entrance. Their first days were spent exploring the city, and making love with abandon. They were intoxicated with the freedom they had to openly express their love in every way possible. No fighting it, no hiding it anymore. Genevieve was glad that they had left the monastery on honest terms with the Abbot.

One day on her own in the marketplace, while smelling various teas and herbs, her hair slipped out from under her cap. The glorious auburn highlights glittered in the sun. Scrambling to tuck her hair back under her cap, she felt a hand take her arm and stop her.

"Stop, please. Let me see the magnificent color of your hair."

"Pardon me, but may I have my arm back!" she answered angrily, as she turned to view her assailant.

Genevieve found a tall, broad shouldered man standing before her. He had a strong chin and well-formed lips. His gold curls fell around his face and his heavy lids sensuously framed his uniquely colored eyes. She had never seen anyone with eyes the color of honey, warm and golden. She felt a liking for this man in spite of the impertinence of his gesture.

"Oh, of course, my apologies. Let me introduce myself. I am Alessandro di Mariano Filipepi, but everyone knows me as Sandro."

"And why must I let you see my hair? What interest could you have in it? That is most indelicate. "

"Let me explain. I am Sandro Botticelli. Perhaps you have heard of me, unless of course you are new to Florence."

"Botticelli, what a funny name: little barrel. But no, I have not heard of you and yes, my... my ...husband and I are new to the city."

She still had trouble calling Evechio her husband , and proud as she was of being his mistress, she also did not like to lie, even to a perfect stranger.

"Well, that explains it. I am Il Botticelli, the well-known artist of Florence, friends of the Medicis. I have had my own painting studio since I was fifteen, so you can gather I have a lot of experience, unless you think me younger than my years."

"The Botticelli? How full of yourself you must be!"

"It is not my title by choice but rather the name my public has given to me. Let me explain. Your hair, it caught the sunlight in such a way and created such a shade of color I have only dreamed of painting. I would love to paint you, use you as the model for my next work: The Primavera. Please say you will at least consider it and come to my studio! Such beauty should not go unrecorded. It should be eternal!"

Genevieve hesitated, unsure of what to do. He seemed like a gentleman and surely if he was an artist, that would explain his improper behavior. To be painted for all the world to see for the ages to come; it made her giddy just thinking of it. And she certainly could use the money.

Evechio might even be proud of her.

Sensing her hesitation, Sandro said "And you can bring your husband with you! My intentions are only artistic, let me assure you, beautiful though you are."

Genevieve blushed and decided in that moment that she would say yes.

"Very well. You win. We will come to your studio and see how and what you paint. When would you like us?"

"Is this afternoon too soon? It is only midmorning and that would give you time to finish your marketing and have your mid-day meal. "

"Very well. I shall tell my husband as soon as I return home."

Happily, Sandro gave Genevieve the directions to his studio and after shaking hands, they parted ways.

When Genevieve returned home, she excitedly addressed Evechio.

"Evechio, sweetheart, I must tell you what happened in the market today. A man stopped me."

"A man did what? Are you alright? How dare he!"

"I'm fine, just fine. He was an artist and he saw my hair when it fell out from under my cap and he said it was a most delightful color and he wishes to paint me!"

"An artist? What are you thinking? He will want you to pose naked. Absolutely not!"

"He said the painting was to be a mythical allegory. I'm sure he sensed that I would not be unclothed! I was ashamed to even have my hair fall from out of my cap. Please, my sweet, can't we at least go to his studio and see his work. Apparently, he is quite well known, even known as The Botticelli. And I would be able to earn some money!"

"It means so much to you?"

"Yes it does. We know no one in this city and it would be a way to meet people too. He seems very easy and friendly."

"You have me, in case you have forgotten!" he answered with an edge in his voice.

She realized she would need to placate him and knew that making love to him was the best thing she could do to soothe his ego. Slowly she removed her cap and shook out her hair. Indeed, it was glorious hair. She smiled at him and began to undo her bodice.

"Are you thinking what I'm thinking?" she whispered drawing close to him and kissing his ear.

"Genevieve, you are incorrigible! But yes, I am always thinking about that when I see you with your hair down and flowing."

He turned and kissed her hard on the mouth and she sensed his ardor. Quickly she disrobed and lay down on their bed, cushioned by their down quilt, as though lying on clouds, she thought. He was upon her in no time, too eager to fully caress her but she was happy to give him the satisfaction and pleasure he so adored.

That afternoon, they made their way through the winding city streets of Florence to Botticelli's studio. Genevieve couldn't get rid of the claustrophobic feel of the narrow streets.

His studio was up a rickety flight of stairs and then, a huge open space facing the north with glass windows as large as she had ever seen. A pretty penny they must have cost, she guessed. Sandro welcomed them both warmly, assessing Evechio's discomfort immediately and doing his utmost to not show too much interest in Genevieve.

"So glad you made it and didn't decide against it. Let me show you some of my paintings so you get a sense of what I do. Artfully, he took them first to a pious Madonna that he was working on. Genevieve gasped in appreciation of the beauty of his work. The woman in his painting was exquisite. Was she really in this league? Nervously she touched her cap to remind herself of her hair.

"What else are you working on?" Evechio asked.

"Well, I have begun my sketches for Primavera. And Mars and Venus. Would you like to see them?"

"Most certainly. I need to know what Genevieve is getting herself into here with you. A man should always look out for his woman."

Evechio's machismo always had a dual effect on her. Secretly she warmed and felt her love for him in her secret spot, and the other side of it irritated her. Did he think she couldn't make up her own mind?

At the side of the room was a table littered with drawings. Sandro picked one up to show Evechio, excluding Genevieve by accident.

"Absolutely not!" she heard Evechio say, startling her with the harshness of his voice.

"What? Let me see. What are you looking at? What's wrong with it?"

Sandro stepped aside so she might take his place next to Evechio. There was the sketch of a man lying half naked in repose and a woman reclining in the other direction. The entire form of her body was apparent from the folds of her gown. Evechio was right, she thought. She could never do this.

"No…no…I'm afraid I could never pose for such a painting. Their relaxed pose, as if they had just been intimate, and her revealing gown. I…I can't do it."

Sandro sighed and said "Never mind, I will simply get 'The Blond' for this one, Venus and Mars."

"The Blond?"

"Yes, The Blond, my latest model. She is not as, what's the word, demure as you. But let me show you some other sketches, the one I must have you for, the Primavera."

Shuffling through his papers, he brought out a large parchment with many figures drawn on it. Three ladies dancing, a woman being whisked away by a man, a girl throwing some flowers and a central figure of a woman.

"This is it, my next masterpiece. Primavera, and I want you to be the woman in the middle, the mother of nature and springtime itself. You will be the central figure and I promise you will be fully clothed, if you insist. But I simply must have your beautiful face and hair for the painting. What do you think?"

Genevieve looked at Evechio and he looked back at her. She had a yearning in her eyes that he recognized and his heart wanted to turn that yearning into joy.

"Alright, I agree. But I must see her in her outfit before you start painting her, just to be sure."

Genevieve quickly kissed his cheek, grabbing his hand and kissing it as well. "Thank you, thank you, thank you, my sweet. I promise you won't be sorry!"

"I can also use her for my Madonna of the Book. I'm sure you would approve of that since it is a pious piece. Now where did I put that sketch?"

He rifled through the papers and finally gave up.

"Well, we can see how this works out and then go from there. Thank you so much for coming but now I must get back to work before the light fades."

"Thank you so much Il Botticelli, when shall I return?"

"Please call me Sandro. If you are to be my model, we will become great friends. Can you start tomorrow? The Blond has not been feeling well so I shall have to concentrate on a different figure for a while and that would be you, my dear."

Genevieve's stomach made a nervous jump at the thought of starting so soon, before she had really gotten used to the idea, mulled it over in her mind, pictured every nuance of it as she tended to do before making any decisions. It reminded her of all the wasted time she's spent mulling over leaving Robert, and yet how quickly she had said yes to Evechio. The heart surely knows, she thought.

They shook hands good-bye and as they turned to leave, Sandro said "Wait, wait, let me see your hair, let me see what I am going to be painting!"

Slowly and reluctantly, Genevieve lifted her hands to her cap. Evechio was the only one she allowed to see her hair flowing completely loose. What would he think? She looked at him but he was looking down at his shoes in discomfort.

"Very well."

She pulled the cap off of her head and her auburn locks fell around her shoulders. She was aware of how short it was compared to the style of the times. She felt strangely naked in front of him, yet it was only her hair. Sandro came forward to touch it but she held up her arm.

"No, No, not yet. I'm not ready. Tomorrow. Wait until tomorrow."

She glanced at Evechio and saw the look of relief in his eyes and she quickly wound her hair back under her cap.

Chapter Two

The next day Genevieve went to work for Botticelli. He began by sketching her face to get a good likeness of her. The real posing had not begun. In one of their conversations, he asked her about Evechio.

"So tell me, Genevieve, about your husband. What does he do all day while you are here?"

"He has no work yet so he explores the city and spends several hours writing, mostly poetry."

"Writing? He knows how to write? That is a special skill. How did he learn that?"

Genevieve thought she shouldn't tell Botticelli about Evechio's time as a monk. It would be awkward and lead to a difficult conversation about their lives. But at the same time, she had mentioned it.

"He worked in a scriptorium when he was in school with the monks in France. He was very accomplished and kept on after his schooling was ended."

As an afterthought she added "He even considered becoming a monk."

"But then he met you! I'm sure your beauty and nature were a huge distraction from the Lord!"

Botticelli laughed at the thought.Genevieve laughed too, happy in the memory of their finally admitting their love for each other.

"But on a more serious note, my patron Lorenzo de Medici has started collecting books for a library. He wishes copies to be made so more of his peers can be educated and informed. Perhaps Evechio would want me to put in a good word to get him work in Lorenzo's workshop? Could he do with the job and the extra income?" Botticelli added.

"Work copying books? Evechio would be thrilled! He would have a chance to read the books he is copying and I know he would adore that. He has a thirst for knowledge. And yes, we most certainly could use the extra income! What a perfect solution! I can't wait to tell him."

Genevieve was clapping her hands and hopping in excitement. How wonderful that her association with Botticelli had proved beneficial to Evechio too! Genevieve's childish excitement made Botticelli wonder about her age. She said she was eighteen years old but something about her made him think she was younger. Why would she lie about her age? She was certainly old enough to be married and away from her family. So why would she hide her youth?

"Very well. I will write a letter of introduction right away before I forget and recommend him for the position in Lorenzo's studio. I'm so glad I can be of help. "

With the letter firmly held against her breast, Genevieve rushed home hoping Evechio was there rather than out and about. She wanted to share the great news as soon as possible. What a cause for a celebration. Genevieve imagined what they could do to celebrate. Perhaps they could dine and drink in an upscale establishment. She could get a new gown, that would please him. He loved to see her in the few beautiful clothes that she owned. They might even afford to buy some Venetian glasses to drink from, and to buy wine on a regular basis.

Genevieve rushed home and found Evechio sitting at the table writing a letter to his mother. The angle of his face in the light made his features sharp and she felt she barely recognized him. Who was this man to whom she had promised her life? It excited her to see another side of him. She wrapped her arms around him from behind and kissed his ear, and worked her way down his neck, savoring the salt of his sweat.

"My love, what are you doing? You are highly distracting!"

"Evechio, I have great news and we must celebrate! Botticelli has written you a letter of introduction to Lorenzo De Medici. He has recommended you for Lorenzo's scriptorium! This means you will have work doing what you love and will be earning an income. Are you pleased?!"

Evechio was delighted. He had been getting restless with nothing to do and no schedule to follow especially after the structured life he had been leading at the monastery. He pushed back his chair and Genevieve nestled onto his lap, her arms around his neck. This, of course, led to kissing which led to passion and soon they were on the bed ready to make love. Gently Evechio moved her on top of him. Much as Genevieve loved the secure feeling of his body sheltering her during love-making, she equally enjoyed being on top and the sense of control it afforded her. This was something utterly new that Evechio had taught her, something her husband had never done. She reveled in the pleasures Evechio had introduced her to in their bed. Her love for him flowed through her and she was filled with joy.

That afternoon, Evechio set out to look into work at Lorenzo De Medici's library. When he returned, he was ecstatic. He had been hired to work copying the wonderful manuscripts Lorenzo had selected.

The next day when Genevieve woke, she found Evechio up already making them some tea. He brought two cups to the bed and she lifted the covers so he would get back in and join her. They drank their tea in silence, enjoying the sun of the morning coming through their window to dispel the gloom of the interior. She knew she had been spoiled by her life in the chateau with its broad windows and wooden polished floors. Here everything was stone, stone and more stone, cold and hard on the feet and the windows were as small as one could get away with, what with the price of glass. But in the morning the eastern exposure of their window allowed them to greet the day with true sunlight. They had their bed placed right in the sunlight's path in order to fully enjoy it each morning. And it gave them a sense of warmth in the morning chill.

With their tea done, it was time to start their day. Evechio gently kissed Genevieve and lying her down, wrapped her up in their quilt so she could stay warm until the heat of the day arrived. She secretly watched him dress, reveling in her good fortune to have such a beautiful man, beautiful in all ways, in her life.

How abysmally different her life would be now if she had stayed with Robert, performing her wifely duties. She had no idea what love-making was until she had met Evechio. With Robert it had been a dreaded and painful humiliation, each and every time. She shuddered at the recollection, shook her head to get rid of the thoughts and continued her secret perusal of Evechio. Too soon he was dressed and ready to go to the scriptorium. What a blessing his talent was, for it would keep them fed and clothed. But now, she reminded herself, she was also contributing to their finances.

Dressed now, Evechio blew her a kiss and headed out the door. Genevieve nestled even further under the covers and lay her arm in the empty place left by Evechio. Life was good, she thought and was soon asleep again.

Genevieve awoke with a start. Why was she feeling so awful and then her dream came flooding back to her: she had gone to Botticelli's studio as asked but found it completely empty but for one huge easel standing in a corner of the room in the shadows, with an enormous painting on it. She called Botticelli's name quietly but got no response. As if compelled, she made her way over to the painting. To her shame, it was a painting of her, lying naked and exposed, her hair spread out around her. Suddenly, to her terror, the figure of Robert stepped out from the shadows. In his hand, she could clearly see that he carried shears. He grabbed her and pressed hard against her. He quickly yanked up her hair as he had done many times before and chopped away at it with a fury.

"How dare you share yourself with another, you are nothing more than a whore, but you are my whore and don't you ever forget that!"

She struggled and called out, but her screams just echoed in the empty room that seemed to grow bigger and bigger until she was swallowed up into nothingness.

Would the nightmares never cease? As long as Robert was alive and well, she would have to live with the fear of discovery and renewed subjugation. She shook herself to be rid of the nightmare and quickly washed and dressed, lastly winding up her hair and donning her cap so she could leave the gloom of the room for the welcome touch of the sun's warmth outside.

She made her way slowly to Botticelli's studio to see when she would be needed. The clock tower struck and she was surprised that it was already eleven o'clock. Half the morning gone. Not that she had anything in particular to accomplish but she still felt a tinge of guilt, knowing how long Evechio had already been up.

Finally at Botticelli's doorway, she hesitated. Pieces of her nightmare clung to her psyche and instilled a moment of fear in her. "Pull yourself together!" she told herself and quickly lifted the latch of the heavy door. Up the stairs she went until she opened up into his studio. Calling gently, she alerted him that she was there as he was painting with his back to her. Without stopping what he was doing, he called her to him, and as she approached, she was startled to see a naked woman lying on the divan. The Blond, she immediately recognized her from the paintings she had seen. Yes, she was just as beautiful in real life as in the paintings. She had such large soulful blue eyes and her hair lay loose about her reaching well passed her waist. Her breasts were firm and her legs long and graceful. Even her fingers had a sense of delicacy and grace. No wonder Botticelli wanted to paint her. How could she, Genevieve, possibly compete? What did he see in her? True, she had always been considered pretty with her auburn hair and green eyes, but her features were small and she felt unremarkable. Of course, Evechio begged to differ but after all, he was in love with her.

"Come over, my dear Genevieve. You must meet Marianna," he said and whispered to her "Better known as The Blond. Not much upstairs but it hardly matters with beauty such as hers."

Genevieve blushed in the embarrassment of seeing such nakedness in front of a man. "I've come at a bad time, I'm sorry to disturb you. I simple wondered what time you expected me here?"

"Yes, of course. Marianna should be completely tired by noon. It will be good to have someone to work with in the afternoon. Come for luncheon and then we will start afterwards." He turned back to the painting and she realized she had been dismissed.

Genevieve quietly descended the stairs, opened the door and slipped out. She was still a little shaken by the episode and the nudity. She had trouble understanding how such women could exist. How could they possibly share such intimacy with a man other than their husband? It still shamed her that Evechio was just her lover and not her husband as of yet. She wondered when they would ever feel free enough of Robert to marry. Would it really be such a sin in the face of God? as Evechio claimed. But she had to respect his wishes when it came to spiritual matters. She had to remind herself that he was atoning for the sin of having broken his vows and having abandoned the church for her sake, not to mention, disappointing his father in his last wishes.

Chapter Three

When Genevieve arrived at the studio, Sandro was finishing his tea, bread and cheese. He offered her a share which she gratefully accepted.

"You are here right on time!" he greeted her. "Let me tell you what I am planning for my next painting." Soon Genevieve got lost in all his plans.

"Time to change into your costume."

He took her to a corner of the large room and pulled back a curtain to reveal a little area that he had set aside as a changing room. On a series of hooks, hung a myriad of gowns, some barely more than a gauzy sheath. He took a white gown off the hook and handed it to her.

"Try this on. I want you clothed in a white under garment. Come out when you are ready and I can start the preliminary sketches. It is an easy pose."

Genevieve hastily undressed and pulled the gown over her head. It clung to her figure in a way that she was not used to. She stepped out of the dressing alcove and made her way towards Sandro.

"Ahem, didn't you forget something?" he said.

She hastily perused her outfit but found nothing missing. He motioned to his head, and she suddenly realized she was still wearing her cap. With a moment of hesitation, she pulled it from her head and unfastened the pins so her luxurious auburn hair fell around her body. The look of pleasure on Sandro's face betrayed his admiration.

"Very well. Let's get to it. I will just be doing more sketches today, to get a sense of your body and its curves in this pose."

Genevieve blushed in spite of herself. He will think I am a silly fool, if everything makes me blush. She climbed on the low platform and struck her first pose as he instructed her. Sandro knitted his brow as he scrutinized her.

"You are much too stiff; you must loosen up. Shake yourself out and try again." But try as she would, she remained too stiff to sketch.

"Alright, do you really want to do this? Are you sure this is for you?" he asked. With panic in her voice, she assured him she wanted to do this.

"Very well, come down and sit in this chair. I will be back in a moment with my secret weapon."

When he returned, he handed her a tankard and she sniffed it warily. It was red wine. He wanted her to drink the entire tankard. Was he trying to drug her? she thought for a second. But his smile was gentle and she decided she trusted him. Slowly she took a few sips, enjoying the fullness of the wine. It had been a long time since she had had the means to enjoy some wine.

She took a few more sips and a sense of relaxation and well-being began to fill her. Half way through, Sandro stopped her, laughing.

"My, you are a cheap drunk! I can see you have already had enough!"

Drunk? So that was his trick. He helped her to her feet and onto the platform. She felt light as a feather.

"Pretend you are in water, like a mermaid." Sandro suggested.

Her limbs flowed as she moved until he told her she was ready. Happily, she took the pose he showed her. With a huge sigh of relief, Sandro picked up his sketching implements and rapidly began sketching without another word. Because he was just doing sketches, she was able to change position frequently, she was glad to see. It was much harder than she had imagined, being so still but he often let her stop and stretch.

"Come and see what I am doing?" he offered her one time.

Eagerly she skipped over to his easel and peered over his shoulder. She let out a gasp and smiled. She looked so delicate and beautiful in the sketches. She had no idea she was so pretty and it secretly pleased her to no end.

"I see you are pleased. Would you like to take a sketch home to Evechio?"

"Could I?! I can't believe you would part with such beautiful drawings! But I would be so pleased to show him what we are doing and to have such a picture of myself!" She clapped her hands in excitement.

"I need to keep this sketch as I think it is the pose I will use for the painting but you can choose from the other sketches. Maybe one standing up and one lying down?"

Genevieve couldn't believe her luck. Here she was being made beautiful and immortal by Botticelli and being paid for it, no less.

Hastily she dressed back into her street clothes and lovingly put the gown she had been wearing for Botticelli back on the rack. Then she gathered up the two sketches and gently held them against herself as she walked home, wondering what Evechio would think.

Back at their room, Evechio was waiting for her, eager to know how her day had gone. Instead of answering, she unrolled the two sketches on the table for Evechio to see. He too gasped at the sight.

"Oh my lord, what on earth? You are almost naked! How dare he! Did he try to molest you in any way? How could you be comfortable posing like that? I'm not sure I approve!"

Genevieve's face fell.

"But don't you think I look beautiful?" she said in disappointment. Looking at her crestfallen face, Evechio regretted his words.

"Of course you look beautiful, because you are beautiful. But couldn't you be dressed in something more substantial? I think I need to have a talk with him!"

"Please Evechio, don't lose your temper with him. He is a good man and treats me with respect. Please, this means the world to me!" Genevieve pleaded.

"We'll see what he has planned for you, then I will decide. Let's leave it at that."

The next day Evechio went to Botticelli's studio with Genevieve.

"Well hello, Evechio, what brings you here to my studio? Did you like the sketches Genevieve took home?"

"Yes, they were magnificent but I am a little concerned by the sheerness of her gown. I simple do not want her to be in a painting in such a revealing manner!"

"Don't worry, my boy, she will look very demure. I needed these sketches to get the form of her body but let me show you the costume in which I plan to paint her. I think you will approve."

He led them back to the changing area and rifled through the rack of clothes. He pulled out a white underdress of muslin with a broad cloth of red velvet. Evechio fingered the cloth and gave a nod of approval.

"This will do," he said to Genevieve's immense relief.

Though Genevieve was happy to be modeling for Sandro, she did find the poses uncomfortable. He was planning a painting that contained many different figures so he needed her to pose in a myriad of ways. For one set of sketches, he brought in two other women for the day to pose with her. They were supposed to be dancing in a circle. Her upraised arms ached and she had trouble keeping her weight on one leg. When it was time for a break, Genevieve hastily donned her robe to conceal her quasi nakedness and was surprised when the other women lounged around in their gauzy outfits. They were barely thick enough to conceal their bodies. She also did stretches, glad to move her body, and rubbed her aching muscles.

"So what do you think about when you are posing?" Sandro asked her. "You have such a contented faraway look in your eyes."

"I think about my husband," she confessed. The word husband slipped easily from her lips now even though it wasn't a truth. The other women exchanged glances and tittered.

"Thinking about your husband, are you? If I thought about my man, Sandro could paint a demon's face from my visage," one woman said and she spat on the floor.

"You must love him very much. And does he love you in return? Can he be trusted or will he be off with the first girl that shows him some leg?" the other woman said, jokingly pulling up her gown to reveal her leg.

Genevieve shuddered involuntarily, thinking of her unhappy days with Robert. "Hit a nerve, did I? said the woman.

"Just some bad memories but not about my husband Evechio. He is as pure as a lamb and I trust him completely," she answered with pride and tenderness in her voice.

"Pure as a lamb!" The woman broke out into laughter.

Genevieve blushed and was sure the women thought she lacked experience and was hopelessly naïve. The more they queried her about her beloved husband, the angrier she got. Finally, she could stand it no longer, listening to their sordid implications.

She turned imploring to Sandro but he appeared to be too busy sharpening his pencils with his knife.

Suddenly Sandro spoke up. "Let the girl have her dreams, her happy ending! What's it to you if she loves her husband? It's just a shame you don't love yours and are chained to him for life. Don't take it out on Genevieve."

So he had been listening. A thought flittered through her mind, the realization that she would be chained to Robert for life, in the eyes of the law and the eyes of God. Chained was the perfect word, but she had managed to break some of those chains, even though it meant living a lie and living in sin.

"I feel sorry for you," she said sincerely to the women. "I wish you could experience what I have experienced about love. But rest assured, I have known the power and brutality of man. But you see, I am still a believer in joy and love.'

With that, Sandro clapped his hands saying "Back to work, my lovelies, back to work! Enough talk about the joys of love and the foibles of men. Perhaps you forget that I am a man!"

Genevieve realized she was reluctant to pose with these jaded, teasing women. But pose she must.

At the end of the day's light, Sandro paid the women and dismissed them with a thank you. As Genevieve gathered up her things to go, Sandro gently stopped her and said," I am happy for you that your life and love is good, but if anything goes wrong, know that you can count on me."

"Nothing can go wrong, nor will it," she answered but she was secretly grateful for Sandro's words. "But I thank you, sir." She bound up her hair and placed her cap on her head and left.

Primavera took many many months to finish. It involved nine figures so there was a lot of posing to be done. But at long last it was finished and the painting was delivered to Lorenzo De Medici for his personal use, to be featured in his palace. Botticelli was thrilled but also sad to say good-bye to a piece he loved so much.

When Botticelli was finally finished with his Primavera, he was eager to start a new painting but with a simpler composition and less figures. Primavera had been a struggle with its nine figures, enjoyable but still a struggle. His new painting was to be of the birth of Venus, Venus rising naked out of the sea with two attendants. He had still not decided who would be the model for Venus. Would it be Genevieve or The Blond?

"My dear Genevieve, I am planning my next painting and would like you to be one of the models. There is the figure of Venus in the center and then two attendants, one on each side of her. I am tempted to use you as Venus, but I have not made up my mind. I will let you know."

Genevieve didn't know what this would entail but she was excited to be in another of Botticelli's paintings! It wasn't till a few days later that she realized the impact of Botticelli's choice. She was walking through the market place when she came face to face with Marianna, The Blond. She was always surrounded by a bevy of men because of her beauty. She motioned for the men to stay back as she approached Genevieve.

Grabbing Genevieve's hand she smiled falsely and tightened her grip, causing Genevieve to cry out.

"What are you doing? You're hurting me?!"

"And well I should, you little tramp. I hear Sandro is considering you for Venus and there is only one way you could be considered over me! You must be sleeping with him! How dare you encroach on my territory. That painting of Venus was to be my crown and glory, to make my beauty immortal. What can Sandro possibly see in you?"

Letting go of Genevieve's hand, she quickly pulled off Genevieve's cap and grabbed her by the hair.

"This is what he loves, your damn hair! He doesn't care about you! So you better give him up or I'll tell your blessed Evechio," she sneered.

She flung back Genevieve's head releasing her hair, turned away and rejoined her bevy of men. Genevieve rubbed her head, gathered her cap up from the ground and hurried home humiliated.

So that's what everyone was thinking, that she was Botticelli's mistress! Evechio would be furious! Pulling herself together, she decided it was time to confront Botticelli.

After her morning shopping, she headed straight to Botticelli's studio and barged in. "Sandro, I'm furious with you! Where are you?" She couldn't see him anywhere.

Suddenly he appeared from behind the screen in disarray. Genevieve was too angry to notice. "How dare you ruin my reputation by expecting me to sleep with you! I love Evechio and am not that kind of girl!"

"Stop your ranting! I was never considering you for Venus. That was always going to be Marianna. She makes the perfect Venus. You will be her attendant, fully clothed by the way."

Genevieve realized that Botticelli was lying but before she could accuse him, Marianna appeared from behind the screen scantily clad. It suddenly all made sense to her. Yes, The Blond was his mistress and as such, was to be featured as Venus in his painting. Botticelli had been good to Genevieve so she decided not to challenge him in front of Marianna.

"Oh, I must have been mistaken, Sandro. I'm sorry to have disturbed you." She quickly turned and left.

Chapter Four

S adly, the flavor of artistry and culture in Florence came briefly but dramatically to an end when Girolamo Savonarola, a Dominican friar, gained power. He managed to take control of the whole city and impose his austerities. Everything changed. Genevieve had seen him once giving a fiery speech and noted that Savonarola had the misfortune of being a very ugly man. His face was marred by pock marks, a testament to the good luck he'd had to survive some childhood illness. His head was partially shaved in the manner of a monk and was smooth in contrast with his face. A huge hooked nose dominated his face coupled with the large lips that formed his mouth. His eyes were small, dark and beady, leaving one with the uncomfortable sensation of being scrutinized when in his presence. He wore the coarse robe of a monk which did nothing to soften his appearance. She marveled that someone with so little charm could hold sway over an entire city as vibrant as Florence had been.

Savonarola was on a tirade. Soon the Bonfires of the Vanities raged throughout the city. People were instructed to discard their cosmetics, mirrors, carnival masks, anything of frivolity. When he began to focus on the art of Florence, in his obsession with religious matters, he decided that all art should be representative of holy images. He went so far as to send his agents from studio to studio to check what art was being done and what paintings were already finished. All work done of mythological figures were to be confiscated and burned.

Botticelli was scrambling to find places to hide his works of Venus and Mars and his other pieces based on mythological themes. Small as Genevieve's lodgings were, he decided that would be a safe enough place to store his masterpieces until Savonarola's passion faded. But he would have to convince Genevieve and Evechio to share their limited space with his works.

The next day, when Genevieve arrived at Botticelli's studio, she found him racing around, stacking some of his paintings in a corner of the floor. He had carefully placed thick pieces of material between each painting to protect each one.

"I am at my wit's end, Genevieve, my wit's end. I must find a safe place for my pieces. Savonarola's men will be coming here for sure in no time and these pieces must be gone! I hear he is even planning on burning the pieces he deems inappropriate! I absolutely must get these out of here and I was hoping you and Evechio could help me," Sandro said broaching the subject with Genevieve.

"Of course we will help! Anything you need!" she answered eagerly. That was exactly what he hoped to hear.

"I was hoping you could store these paintings in your lodgings. No one would think to look there, what with Evechio being known for his rendition of sacred texts." responded Sandro.

"At our place?" stammered Genevieve. She was trying to imagine where and what a responsibility this would be. "I can't imagine..." she began but stopped herself short.

She started to see what an honor this would actually be, to have the master's paintings in residence in their space. She thought about hanging them on the walls or storing them in the loft space.

"Yes, of course we will. It will be a great honor and responsibility for us and I am honored that you would trust us with such precious things as your art!"

Sandro gave a huge sigh of relief and in his gratitude, he embraced her.

"We will have to carry them at night, I'm afraid. I'm sorry to take up your time then."

"It is just fine, I promise we will come here later in the evening, when the streets are empty."

When Genevieve returned home that evening, she greeted Evechio by the door with a pleading look on her face.

"My dear one, I have a favor to ask you. You have heard about Savonarola's new and dreadful policy about non-sacred art. Sandro is heart-broken that he may have his mythological paintings taken away and even burned. He has asked that we store them here for the time being. Just think what an honor it would be! To have Botticelli's in our home! I know our space is small but we could hang a couple and store the others in the loft." Genevieve pleaded with her hands in a supplicating clasp.

Evechio stopped to think of the feasibility of the request. They could not afford to lose Botticelli's employment and his friendship. As well, Evechio was utterly disgusted and appalled by what Savonarola was doing to the art world: to actually be burning paintings!

"Of course we must help him save his paintings!"

Genevieve embraced him and explained the need to go to the studio this evening, late. "No ale for me tonight, for I would fall asleep. I must stay awake!" Evechio said.

"I am so glad you agreed to this! I was a little alarmed when he first suggested it, but then I realized what an honor and how important this was," responded Genevieve.

They made a hasty dinner and began to clear the space in the loft for the paintings.

"You know this means we can have no one come into our home during this time. Are you willing?" Evechio said.

"Yes, I will forgo my chats with the neighbors, our tea times together. I will have to go to their places instead." she replied.

Later that evening, they dressed in their plainest and darkest clothes, so as not to draw attention to themselves. They made their way to Botticelli's and were grateful that the moon was not full. Botticelli greeted them at the door, and with apprehension in his voice, asked if anyone had seen them.

Reassured by their answer, he handed Genevieve the smaller of his paintings, all wrapped in material and gave Evechio the larger ones.

They silently descended the stairs and entered into the street, looking both ways. They moved as quickly as possible and were grateful that they lived so close to his studio. But on their street, a drunken man with his arms around two ladies of the night, was winding his way down the narrow street towards them.

"Well, hello there, what have we here?" the drunken man exclaimed.

"Out so late and with such a load to carry. What is this?" He moved to block the narrow street each time Genevieve and Evechio tried to pass.

"Shhh" Genevieve couldn't help herself from saying. "Do be quiet or you will wake the neighbors."

"Oh, a brave little lady to be out so late, and yet you don't look like a lady of the night" he continued.

By then Evechio was losing his patience. "Stand aside before I make you," he expostulated.

"My, my, what a temper on such a lovely evening. Why not join us in our fun. The girl is certainly a comely lady and I would pay her well for her services."

That was the last thing he said before Evechio put down his paintings and pushed the man down onto the street.

"Enough of your talk. Don't insult my wife with your ugly suggestions and get out of our way!" Evechio whispered loudly and harshly.

The man slowly clambered to his feet with the aid of the two women who were clucking over him and hoping their evening was not over yet as they were hoping to earn a pretty penny. The drunken man lunged at Evechio, but he stepped aside and the man hit the wall.

"You bastard!" he shouted. Evechio realized they were going to be in serious trouble if the neighbors came out and wondered what they were doing.

"Look my man, I'm sorry. Let me help you!" he said in a solicitous tone of voice.

Taken aback by Evechio's change in attitude, he allowed him to take him by the arm and lead him back to the women, who eagerly took charge of him. Evechio stooped to pick up his load and whispered to Genevieve to come quickly, letting her pass in front of him.

At their abode, they worked their way up the narrow stairs with their unwieldy packages and were grateful, sighing in relief when they finally closed the door behind them.

"We will leave them here against the wall for now and go right to bed," Evechio suggested. Genevieve agreed and soon they were sound asleep, exhausted by their escapade.

At first Botticelli had been horrified by Savonarola's "purification" of the city. Especially as his works of art were a target for Savonarola's distaste. The sensual transparent draping of his female figures and languid postures of his men were a direct invitation to Savonarola's criticism, and this didn't even compare to the subject matter of his paintings: figures from Greek mythology. But Botticelli realized that to survive, he would have to change his style and subject matter. Paintings of the Madonna littered his studio now. His models, instead of being draped in diaphanous gauzy gowns that clung to their forms, were clothed in rich modest garments, with pious expressions on their faces. They were still distractingly beautiful, but the subject matter was now acceptable to the Florence of Savonarola.

When Savonarola finally fell out of favor, and was led to his execution, there were few who mourned his passing. He was hanged and burned as a heretic. He had gone too far and out stayed his welcome and the people hoped to regain the joyful and artistic flavor that had previously inhabited Florence. They were done with austerity and condemnation. They wanted to stroll along the streets with ease, and enjoy the sensuous pleasures of secular art and music. Yes, perhaps they had strayed too far from the church but Savonarola had gone too far in the opposite direction. Rather than mourn his passing, the people mourned the destruction of the innumerable works of art and writing that had been sacrificed to Savonarola's ideology and religious fervor, and they were glad to be rid of him.

PART FIVE:
Return

Chapter One

Genevieve was on her way to Botticelli's studio for a sitting. It was a beautiful autumn day, the sun shining and the air crisp. The trees were changing colors and she thought of the beauty around her. She was infinitely content. She was almost there when she heard:

"La Voila, prennez la!"

She was startled to hear a loud French voice and even more startled by the words "There she is. Grab her!" Before she had time to turn around, strong hands grabbed her arms and wrenched them behind her back. Her wrists were hastily tied with rope and before she could catch her breath and call out, her mouth was gagged. She struggled madly. Momentarily breathless, she looked up and saw the face of her assailant. And her heart broke. Her husband stood before her with such anger in his eyes, she feared for her life. The day she had so dreaded had come, he had found her. But how?

He yanked off her cap so her hair fell wildly around her face. He grabbed her face so she had to look at him. She shut her eyes tight, wishing and praying him away. He pushed her along down the street with the help of his men. They soon stopped and she was thrown into a carriage while Robert sat across from her, firmly holding the rope that confined her. Slowly he closed his eyes and then took a deep breath. Finally he spoke:

"How did you dare desert me!? I knew one day God would answer my prayers and return you to your rightful place as my wife. You wonder how I found you? You never thought I would find you here, when you had yourself painted in all your likeness? What a fool you are. You didn't stop to think that I know people here in Florence. Don't you remember the Count Rudolpho? He came to a hunting season with us, and took quite a fancy to you if I remember. Said he'd never forget your beautiful face and the exquisite color of your hair. Well, he didn't forget and he happened to see a painting at the Medici's palace last month. And there you were. He said he would have known it was you, just by the color of your hair. He immediately wrote me and alerted me to the fact that you must be here in Florence. I had been praying for something like this! Finding out where Botticelli's studio was, I realized you might be coming and here you are! Enfin!!! Finally!!!" he muttered and appeared to go to sleep.

Genevieve was terror stricken and unbelieving. How could God have allowed this to happen? She doubted Robert was planning to kill her. He might be a brute but not a murderer. If he was that angry, he would have done it then and there. He obviously had something else in mind for her. What would Evechio think! He would not know where she was and why she was gone. He'd be heart sick. What if she thought she had abandoned him? What if he thought she was dead? What would he think, feel? Her heart ached for him. Tears streamed down her face.

She couldn't contain her sobbing and with the gag in her mouth, she gurgled and gasped.

Robert opened his eyes at the sound. They were outside of the city limits by now. If Genevieve had looked up, she would have seen a look of concern on Robert's face but she could not bring herself to look at the man who was destroying her life for a second time. Robert stood up and slowly loosened the gag in her mouth. She was able to gasp for air and breathe easier. She couldn't help herself. She looked up in hopes of seeing what Robert was thinking. But his lidded blue eyes took on their enigmatic shadowed look that she had found so frustrating.

She tried screaming with the loosened gag. Robert's reaction was instantaneous. He pulled a vial out of his bag, pulled her head back and shoved the vial passed the gag into her mouth, letting every drop of the vial's liquid go down her throat. What was it, she worried? What would happen to her?

Robert saw the fear in her eyes and exclaimed, "It's just a sleeping draught to calm you down! What kind of monster do you take me for?!" and flung himself angrily back in his seat.

A sense of relief, coupled with a warmth created by the draught, made her lean back and slowly let the tension out of her aching body. Before she knew it, she felt herself letting go, drowsy, warm, tired, ancient, weary…

When Genevieve was finally fully asleep, Robert took her slumped form and lay it down on the carriage seat. He unbound her wrists and gently put a blanket over her after neatly arranging her gown. He looked down at his wayward wife and try as he might to hate her, an unusual and unexpected tenderness filled his heart as he gazed at her seemingly innocent beauty. No one had ever made him feel this way, he reflected. She was who God had intended for him, he was certain. He leaned down and kissed her forehead and then settled down in his seat for a much needed nap.

When Genevieve awoke, she was tied to a bed, gagged again. The blessed draught had allowed her aching body and heart to sleep but now upon awaking, she relived the horror of the past events and struggled to release herself. Robert appeared above her and told her they were only a day away from the chateau.

"You slept for twelve hours. We are taking a rest and some supper at a hostelry and would be setting out again in a few hours. Enjoy the bed. It is soft and comfortable, unlike the carriage. If you promise not to scream, I will feed you some supper."

Genevieve nodded. She realized there was no hope for her now. Not until she could be on her own, untied. Robert brought a bowl of soup over to the bed and slowly fed her the hearty stew it contained.

"Please" she begged in a voice made hoarse by the gag, "Please Robert, let me go. I don't love you and I won't ever make you a good wife. You deserve a real wife. Please let me go!"

She looked pleadingly into his eyes but only saw his own passion and anger.

"Never, you are my wife in the eyes of God! There is no one else for me, from the first moment I saw you as a young girl at the chateau, I knew you were made for me. You will learn to be a good wife. You will learn!"

The only comfort she got was from the thought that Robert didn't know about Evechio. He had found her alone on the street and his friend Rudolpho wouldn't have known much about her. Evechio would be safe from harm at least, even if his heart would be broken. She tried with all her strength to send a message from her mind to his, hoping it might reach from heart to heart:

"Evechio, I am alive. I am with Robert on my way to the chateau where we lived. I love you!"

Perhaps he would hear. Perhaps he would know what to do. She drank heavily of the wine from the tankard Robert put to her lips. She wanted the deadening that would come from too much wine. She wanted to feel empty inside. Robert laughed at her eager drinking.

"Trying to get drunk, my dear? You know what that does to me. But I will leave you alone in that way until we are properly reunited at the chateau as man and wife. The priest will come and give us his blessing, he promised. You will need to go to confession and do penance, of course."

After finishing the wine, Genevieve lay down and curled up into a ball. Robert lightly gagged her as a precaution. He covered her with the blanket and left her to cry herself to sleep.

Chapter Two

After such a long ride, Genevieve and Robert finally arrived back at the outskirts of the chateau. They approached the gates and the caretaker quickly ran out to unfasten the ornate lock for them. Yet more constraints, thought Genevieve. She sighed deeply and Robert scrutinized her face. They rode along the avenue bordered by the beautiful chestnut trees of the autumn. The shiny brown nuts in their prickly cases lay scattered upon the ground. Genevieve longed to hold the smooth nut in her hand. She felt its smoothness would soothe her after all the roughness of the trip.

Once they arrived at the chateau itself, Genevieve groaned inwardly at the realization she was now a prisoner in her former home, a home that had once held some very happy memories before her marriage to Robert. With her hands still tied in front of her, Robert pulled her from the carriage, grabbing her as she fell. The feeling of his arms around her infuriated her. The huge wooden front door stood open to receive her, entrap her, she thought. It would slam behind her and that would be that. Meanwhile various people had assembled there, people she did not know, people who three years ago did not live at the chateau. Would there be any familiar faces? What of the midwife, Therese? Did she still live in the village or had she had to flee too?

"Jacques, come here and take my woman to her chambers. She will need a long hot bath and then time to rest. Do not let her out of your sight, ever! Matilde will guard her in her bath but you must stay in the outer chamber," ordered Robert.

"Yes, my lord! I fully understand my job in this matter," he replied solemnly.

Genevieve looked at the man who was her new "guardian". He was a big man with a severely twisted back, a hunchback, she realized. His enormous hands were calloused and covered in hair. He clutched the rope that was her lead and proceeded through the doors without a backward glance. Whether she would be safe with this man, she did not know but she knew he was his master's servant. She had seen the look of devotion on his face when he had addressed Robert. Perhaps Robert was the only person who had ever treated him with respect, not revulsion at his misshapen form.

Once in her chamber, Jacques pulled out a set of keys on a ring, and locked the door. She had a moment of apprehension until she heard a woman's voice come from the bathing chamber.

"Jacques, is that you? Bring the mistress here so she might take a bath, and bring more wood for the fire so I may heat up more the water," said a woman's voice. He indicated the door to the next room and then he left the room, locking the door after himself.

Timidly, Genevieve made her way to the bathing chamber and peering around the door, she saw a large, round woman, bending over the fire with a big kettle in her hands. Grunting, the woman turned to face the metal tub that was positioned as close to the fireplace as possible. After pouring the boiling water into the narrow tub, she looked up, wiping the steam from her reddened face.

"Well, what are you waiting for?" she asked sternly. "I don't bite, unless, of course, I'm ordered to. Come here while I untie your hands. Then into the bath. You are filthy after your trip home! It's a wonder that the master would even want such a dirty fright back in his house, let alone in his bed."

She shook her head as she untied the ropes, and her graying hair that had escaped her cap, bobbed with the motion.

Genevieve was so relieved to have her hands free of the ropes, and she plunged them into the bath water to soothe them. Matilde pulled her roughly around and began to unlace her dress. Being naked in front of a stranger was the last thing on Genevieve's mind, she was so eager to climb into the bath. She couldn't help but give a huge sigh of pure relief and even pleasure as the warm water enveloped her.

"I'll leave you there to soak for a time so the grime will come off more easily. Jacques will be back with more wood soon to keep the fire going. It wouldn't do to have you catch a chill and die after all the trouble the master had in finding you and bringing you back to your rightful place in the eyes of God. That he can forgive you is beyond me! But I'll not have your death on my conscience." Muttering to herself, she proceeded to a bench at the side of the room and took up a basket of knitting.

Genevieve was too comfortable to care what the woman was muttering about. After she had soaked for some time, Matilde added more hot water and began to scrub Genevieve with a cloth and soap.

"Ouch, you're hurting me! Let me do that!" protested Genevieve. "I won't have any skin left after you are done.

"Do hush, my lady, I won't have the master sharing his company with a girl covered in even a spot of dirt!"

So saying, she dunked Genevieve under the water to wet her greasy hair, then worked her fingers on Genevieve's scalp.

They heard the outer door unlock and knew Jacques was back with a load of wood. "Just leave it there," Matilde called and he retreated, locking the door once again.

Once the bath cooled, Genevieve was pulled from the tub and wrapped in towels and placed on a stool by the fire while Matilde carried the wood in from the outer room.

When Genevieve was dry and warm, Matilde led her to her bed chamber where a fresh sheath and gown lay on the bed. Stockings and shoes were there too but no cap for her head.

"Where is my cap?" asked Genevieve.

"The master doesn't want your hair covered. He says it is too beautiful to conceal. We will braid it and ornament it, but not cover it."

"But... but... I must cover it!" and Genevieve couldn't help thinking to herself: 'Only Evechio should be free to see the beauty of my hair!' and realizing yet again her predicament, she burst into tears and threw herself on the bed.

"My lady, that is no way to behave. You have sinned deeply in the eyes of God and now the master has granted you the opportunity to repent and take up your rightful place at his side! Most men would not be so generous!"

Genevieve was indeed grateful that she was alive but only so that one day she could escape and make her way back to the man she loved, Evechio. Robert was sorely mistaken if he thought she would be a good wife in any meaning of the word.

"Hurry now, the master is waiting for you to join him for a quiet supper. It is getting late."

They made their way through the familiar corridors but nothing of its familiarity comforted her. In the main hall, a small table had been set up by the fireplace with two settings. Reluctantly, Genevieve took a seat and accepted a glass of wine from the young woman who was serving them. She ate a few mouthfuls while Robert proceeded to stuff himself with meats and breads. He tried to get her to converse with him but she uttered as little as possible.

"How was your bath, a welcome relief, I'm sure after our long voyage? Matilde has done a good job of cleaning you up and adorning your hair."

He reached across the table to touch one of her curls that had escaped from the braids. Genevieve flinched involuntarily.

"Listen, Genevieve," Robert began in an icy tone. "You are mine, do you understand, mine then and mine now, and it will never be any different until the day I die. I assure you that you will never be out of my sight or control again. I am your husband and master in all things, in the law and in the sight of God! The sooner you embrace this, the better for all of us! Do you understand?"

"No I don't! I didn't ask for any of this. You took me as your wife against my will and I will never, never love you or be your wife in the true sense of the word. Only Evechio will be!" Genevieve burst out before she could help herself. At the name Evechio, Robert jumped from his seat and banged the table. She was afraid he would harm her in his anger but he stayed where he was.

"You love another?! Don't you ever speak that name again or you will be sorry," he growled. Without waiting to see her reaction to his outburst, he stomped from the room.

As soon as Robert left the room, Jacques appeared. He must have been stationed there. He grabbed her roughly by the hand and took her back to her room where he locked her in for the night. Matilde was waiting to undress her, removing her gown and undoing her hair. Genevieve pushed Matilde away as she went to brush Genevieve's hair. That was only for her or Evechio! she thought. She resolved to never allow anyone else to ever brush her hair, in memory of Evechio.

Comforted only slightly, she brushed her hair and braided it for the night, aching for Evechio and their evening ritual. After she lay her head on the pillow, Matilde blew out the candle and retreated to the other chamber for the night. In spite of all, Genevieve fell rapidly asleep in the comfort of a real bed.

Chapter Three

B eing home in the chateau again left Genevieve with night-mares every night. Robert gave her the courtesy of her own chamber but had a guard standing by the door. She would wake from her nightmares in a sweat, full of tears of despair. What must Evechio be thinking? She ached for him and his loving ways. All she could think about was how to return to him but she was guarded at all times and the stables were under lock and key. She knew there was nothing she could do.

Now that Genevieve was returned to Robert, she knew there would be some retribution for her desertion and long absence. She was sure he was torn between a burning curiosity to learn where she had been and how she survived and the over-riding need to be cold and punitive towards her, as if her return was not welcome. In the beginning he spoke to her not at all and never looked her way. Occasionally he barked orders to her.

Genevieve noted after a couple of weeks had passed, that Robert had not insisted on performing his husbandly duties at night. She was grateful for the time to prepare herself but at the same time, every night, she didn't sleep a wink waiting for his intrusion into her bed chamber. She slept fitfully and was plagued with nightmares and dreams of sorrow and anguish, remembering Evechio.

She had also noticed that Robert had stopped drinking entirely and his nature was much improved because of it. His surly, lustful, violent temperament had all but disappeared, much to her relief. After a couple of weeks, he was almost courteous with her. Of course there was resentment on his part that she had left him but he seemed to have forgiven her for the most part, and was content with the way things were now. His improved behavior helped ease some of Genevieve's pain.

Soon after her arrival, Genevieve had noticed that she was ravenous yet queasy. How could she be both? When she missed her monthly bleeding, she suddenly realized she must be with child, and with Evechio's child! She was filled with such a mixture of emotions: elated that she was carrying Evechio's child and heartbroken that he would not be able to share in her joy. Each morning and night she sent a silent prayer to Evechio hoping with all her heart that he would feel it:

"My love, I miss you so much, your warmth, your touch, the security and tenderness of your embrace. Please come for me, my dearest! I am carrying your child, YOUR child. Can you imagine how wonderful that feels yet how sorrowful that you aren't here to share this with me!"

Then panic set in when she considered Robert in the equation. Would he accept another man's child? She knew he was desperate for an heir. Should she be honest with him or trick him? For a few days she pondered her decision. She finally came to the conclusion that she needed to pretend the child was his for its own protection. She realized it meant sleeping with him again and she braced herself for this necessary encounter.

That night at supper she drank more than usual. She felt she needed the extra fortitude and numbing that wine brought her. She remembered her taste of wine in Botticelli's studio. It had helped to free her. Perhaps it would help now. Robert seemed unaware of her added consumption of alcohol, much to her relief.

After dinner was finished, while she still felt brave enough, she went to Robert as he sat in his chair, and put a hand on his arm.

"Robert, you have changed, I can see that. You have respected the sanctity of my bedchamber and I have appreciated that. I think the time has come that I live as your wife again. May I join you in your bed tonight?"

Robert was shocked but quickly showed his happiness by taking her hand and kissing it gently.

"Yes, I was a brute in the past but I have truly learned my lesson. I simply couldn't bear to live without you. I need you to see the new me now that I don't drink or gamble. I lead a simple, healthy life and I want you to see the new man I've become. Perhaps in time you might even come to love me."

He blushed unable to look up into her face. He kissed her palm and stood up, keeping her hand in his. Together they wove their way to his bedchamber.

When she was younger, she hadn't known it could be any other way than Robert's idea of love-making, but now she knew better. She realized she no longer needed to experience pain when she knew how much pleasure this very act provided if a little tenderness was involved. No, she wouldn't benefit by being a victim, by resisting him when the odds were always hopeless. She would have to live with this man on his terms and so she must make them her terms as well.

She pulled his face down to hers, and opened her lips. As she had hoped, Robert was totally startled by this change of events. Now she stood a chance, now she could take control and make-love her way, and they might never have to go through the fighting again.

"On your back, on your back," she cooed as she wrapped her legs around him. Slowly, ever so slowly, she rolled him over until she was arched over his chest with her tongue playing on his lips. As he became more passionate, she remembered clearly the moments of terror she had felt as a young girl, the fear and the pain. It was as if all the years had melted away and she was back in those times. Fortunately, before it became unbearable, Robert was done and she rolled off of his sweating body and curled up in the sheets. He sighed with pleasure and turned away from her to get some sleep. Thankful that his attentions were over, she wept to herself until sleep came to her.

Robert's eagerness for her returned the following night and the night after that. She went through the motions, thinking solely of the child she was carrying. When would she be able to tell him she was with child? Perhaps the midwife could be bribed to tell him that love making was not healthy during pregnancy.

A couple of weeks later she decided it was time to tell Robert. At breakfast, feeling sick to her stomach, Robert asked if she was unwell. It provided the perfect opportunity to tell him the news.

"Robert, I have been feeling unwell in the mornings and would like to see the midwife. I believe I am going to have a child. "

She could not bring herself to look at him. Instead, she looked down at her belly where she had placed her hand.

"A child! My child!" Robert leapt up from his chair and ran to her side kneeling by her chair. He placed his hand on her belly.

"My love, you have made me the happiest man in the world. I could not love you more! Yes, we must get the midwife immediately. Everything must be done right to insure a healthy birth."

Everything went as Genevieve planned. The new midwife, Bernice was willing to say that the pregnancy was precarious and intercourse should be abstained from. The months passed and Genevieve fell into a welcome routine that helped her overcome her grief. She walked daily, guarded still, and often sang to her unborn child. She knitted and sewed all manner of items for the baby.

Chapter Four

S oon after the announcement of her pregnancy, Robert decided
to celebrate with a fancy dinner party. Robert insisted that she
adorn herself in her most luxurious satin gown. He was having
important friends to dine that evening and she must be a credit to
his name or hell was to pay. She was not a child anymore and knew
that this was the moment to obey because it was a simple enough
request. Juliet, her maid servant, helped "Madame la Viscountess"
with her toilette, first preparing a delightful soapy bath which
relaxed all the tension right out of every one of Genevieve's pores.
While Juliet massaged her scalp, she could feel the tension she
carried blocked between her brows melt away.

Artfully, Juliet pinned Genevieve's hair up into a delicate bun
and fashioned the front into tightly curled bangs that framed her
face. A few delicate tendrils of hair curled down from the bun,
gently caressing her neck as they wound around to the front to rest
upon her bare shoulders. Powders were applied to her face to cover
the effect that the sun had left upon it, and a harsh red was used
to sharpen the angles of her cheeks, and the paleness of her lips.
Her eyelashes were spikes of black after completion. She blushed
in shame imagining what Evechio would think if he could see her
now. How false, how artificial, how could the educated have such
poor taste, such poor judgment of beauty? She shuddered in mild

revulsion. This was her life now, this was her look and she had better get used to it!

"Madame is cold?"

"Non, non, Juliet, not at all."

"Ah non, good, then perhaps she is dissatisfied with my work? I have done something wrong? It is not the latest fashion from Paris?"

Juliet became more and more distressed as she went on. "I asked Claudette, who was just there with Madame la Baron last week and this is what she showed me and...and..."

"No, Juliet, I am sure this is exactly how it should be. It is just strange to me that we must imitate beauty that has strayed so much from nature's wonderful palette. Don't you agree? For instance, put your face next to mine and look in the mirror. Your natural beauty is infinitely more pleasing and soothing to the eye than the harshness of my face, don't you think?"

"But of course not, Madame, don't be silly, I am no beauty the way you are. Though my father insists I am the loveliest of his daughters." Juliet laughed ruefully "But only because I am his only daughter as he's so kindly reminds whomever he is talking to. But I have thought long and hard about this and perhaps beauty would be a burden. When a lad comes calling for me, I know it is not my beauty he is interested in and therefore his interest will not fade as my beauty does. There is a certain comfort in that, I think."

She smiled secretly and blushed as she completed her sentence and Genevieve realized Juliet must indeed have experienced this first hand in her own life.

"Oh Juliet... you must have met the man who taught you this lesson first hand, I can tell!"

"Oh Madame, you can tell?"

"Of course! Being in love myself, I know all the signs. It is too wonderful of a feeling to hide. You should speak about it as much as possible and share it with someone who cares for you! You should..."

Genevieve stopped dead in her sentence realizing that she had shared her most precious secret, shocked at how easily she had done so.

"Madame, you in love! After all these years of marriage? Then why did you leave him? He must be a happy man to not only have you back, but so in love, such a young and beautiful wife as you are!"

In love with Robert? How could Juliet have made such a mistake? She had been a child then, a child! Not even thirteen and he was a man of thirty. What does a child at that age know of the love between a man and a woman, the passion that can arise, the tenderness?

The dinner was a great success. She was beautiful and behaved the part of a devoted and attentive wife and she could see Robert's admiration in his eyes as he introduced her to each of the guest as they arrived.

Halfway through the dinner, Monsieur Leveque raised a glass of burgundy glowing wine, sparkling in the candle light, and turning to Robert exclaimed, "Mon Cher, what a delightfully beautiful and intelligent wife you have acquired for yourself! What a find! And why on earth was I not invited to the wedding, my friend? Did you sneak off to Paris and abduct this divine apparition on your last trip? Why I was here three months ago and knew nothing of this young lady. Do you tell us how you met and what great love drove you to such a hasty and secretive marriage?!"

At first Robert was dreadfully taken aback. How would he answer this awkward prying old man? But he managed to weasel out of having to think fast on his feet by turning towards Genevieve, and she saw the anger in his eyes and tightening of his lips as he looked at her. He too raised his glass of water in her direction and said:

"Yes, a toast to my discovery, my creation actually. I simply cannot tell in what circumstances I found my wife before we met. Perhaps I should not tell in mixed company, if you catch my meaning."

He sneered, and chuckled, exchanging glances with the men in the crowd.

"But where should I begin this tale of poverty and destitution?" again he winked at the company and they snickered understandably. "Actually, I knew her as a child and to save her from poverty, I married her at a young age. But Genevieve had a mind of her own. She decided she would do better on her own even after all the money and concern I spent on her education and health. She tried to live on her own for several years but realizing her folly has come back to me. And being such a forgiving and understanding man, I have waited for her and never asked her what she did those years to keep bread in her mouth. Ah, am I not the perfect husband?"

His eyes had narrowed into the thinnest slits and the sneer deepened on his face as he turned to Genevieve in triumph. Oh yes, he seemed to be saying to her, just try to get out of this one, this one that you so deserve! Now all of my lecherous friends will be harassing you, leering at you, disrobing you with their eyes. Live with that humiliation just as I've lived with the humiliation of your departure!

Yes, Robert had won this round, everything about her behavior would fit in with his story perfectly and now she understood why he had insisted on such a garish display of jewelry, make-up and such a low cut bodice on her gown! She indeed was utterly humiliated but her humiliation would be twice as complete if she allowed him to see this. All she wanted in the world was to run from the room to remove the distasteful garments and baubles, scrub every inch of her skin, hide, cry, scream in her shame and anger! But she knew she would never live down the humiliation if she did.

So calmly she lifted her glass to meet his across the table and smiling every so humbly, she said "Please gentlemen, ladies, let us not toast my beauty but rather the generosity and compassion of the man I have as my husband. For three years I worked, it is true, but not to avoid my commitment to my husband, but rather to be more worthy of him. I too wanted to learn devotion and compassion, as he was an example of both, so I worked in an orphanage in southern France, learning the virtues of giving, taking the education that had been so generously given to me and returning it to the world. And not only was I a teacher, but I also was learning how to be a good mother. When the occasion arises, I wanted be more than prepared. I wanted to be sure to be the best wife and mother I could, because my husband deserves no less."

Ah, she had had the effect she desired. The women were looking with kind glances her way and the men seemed ashamed, looking awkwardly at their laps. As for Robert, she could see a mixed emotion of intensified anger that shot at her like bullets and an element of admiration for her quick thinking. She was no fool, he could tell, no, she was no longer the terrified helpless girl he had tormented for those three years. She had become his match.

As the guests were leaving, she and Robert stood arm and arm at the door, for form's sake waving until the last carriage drove off. She hastily disengaged herself from his heavy grasp.

"I think I'll go upstairs to get out of this cumbersome outfit now that your dinner party is over."

As she turned to head up the stairs, he grabbed her hand, detaining her. What now? she thought. Her entire body tensed itself against his intrusion.

"Quite a performance, my dear little wife!"

Before he could go on, she hurried upstairs as quickly as possible. Once behind closed doors in her bedchamber, she felt almost joyful. Not only did she have the rest of the evening to relax, she had outsmarted Robert. She had created an honorable past for herself and made a good impression on Robert's friends, and she might even become friends with one or two of the younger wives! Oh, how she wanted a true friend, like Delphine, like Evechio!

She sat in front of her mirror, dreaming, and unfastening her hair. The room was filled with the pinkish glow of her candles and her lacy nightgown already lay on the silk coverlet of her bed. How cozy, how inviting! She would curl up and think of her beloved Evechio. She would allow herself this treat tonight. Perhaps she might even dream of him in all his glory throughout the night. She quickly crawled into bed.

Just as a sigh escaped her lips, she heard the creak of her door and there stood Robert. He locked the door, never taking his glance off her face.

"Robert," she began as she sat up. "Robert…" she stammered again, "I thought you were going to have a quiet night alone, my dear? Has the fire gone out? We could get Jaques to rebuild it, if you would like?"

"Being alone doesn't suit a married man, ma chere. You were brilliant tonight. I can't contain myself. I must have you!"

He lay down onto the bed next to her. She had forgotten his forcefulness, his strength. And she hadn't forgotten his anger. She sensed she had to do as he said. At some point he had wrestled himself out of his shirt and she was aware of hair and sweat pressing against her. As he kissed her, he used his free hand to unbuckle his pants and free himself of its prison, ready to start.

"Robert, I am not in the mood! I feel sick all the time with the pregnancy and the midwife said that being with you in that way could harm the baby. We can't take that chance. Please, go to your own room."

Robert looked angry and then chagrinned.

"You are right, the baby is the most important thing in our lives right now."

With a deep sigh, he redressed and lifted himself from her bed after giving her a kiss good-night. Genevieve breathed deeply with relief and felt reassured that he would not bother her again.

Chapter Five

Genevieve sensed that the time for her confinement was approaching. The baby inside her was very restless. Genevieve had many nights of poor sleep which left her looking less than her best. Robert had kept his word to not require her to sleep with him in any way. He had told her, she was not attractive to him in that condition, especially with the added weight she had put on. Genevieve's relief was profound. She had been spared his attentions from the minute she had declared herself pregnant. But she knew the baby's early arrival would be suspect. That with the physical experience of childbirth left her worried and added to her sleepless nights.

At last, the time came. She was getting up from the table after her morning meal with Robert, when she felt an extreme cramp. She staggered back into her chair.

"What's wrong?!" Robert asked jumping up from his chair. He ran to her side and knelt down to see her face. It was drawn with pain and beads of sweat had appeared on her brow.

"A cramp, it might be time, Robert. Please send for Bernice right away! I will need help from the midwife with this first baby."

"But it's too early! You are not due for a month. Are you sure?"

"I'm sure! Please Robert, help me upstairs and send for the midwife," Genevieve said as calmly as possible.

As Robert helped her to her room, another contraction doubled Genevieve over in pain. She sat down on the steps until she could gather her strength. Robert sat with her and placed his hand on her belly.

"I can feel the baby moving!" he said in wonder. "Let's pray it's a boy!"

On they went and Robert helped her out of her clothes and onto the bed in her chemise. It was summer and the room was warm. A slight breeze was coming in the windows and Genevieve was grateful. After Robert saw her settled in, he ran downstairs to send for Bernice.

All sorts of scenarios wove through Genevieve's mind. What if she died? She would never see Evechio again. Who would take care and love their baby? Would Robert realize the truth? What would he do? Force her to give up the baby? Maybe he would release her too and she could return to Florence and find Evechio! Such good and bad thoughts came and went between contractions.

Soon Bernice, the midwife, was there. Genevieve gave a huge sigh of relief. She would tell her everything. If only Robert would leave!

"Robert, I need to talk with Bernice about women things. Would you mind going to get some milk for me. I'm thirsty," she said as sweetly as possible.

When he was gone, she turned to Bernice, grabbing her hand.

"Quick, you must listen to me! You see that the baby is a month early which would be a great worry, but in fact the baby is right on time. It is not Robert's baby and I am so worried he might harm the baby when and if he finds out. Please stay with me for as long as possible. Say you need to watch me for a few days because it was a difficult delivery! Please!"

Bernice squeezed her hand in reassurance.

"Yes, of course, my dear. Rest your mind and heart. I will do everything necessary to protect you and the baby. My sister will be joining us. She always comes when I deliver babies in case of complications so between the two of us, you and the baby will be protected."

A few minutes later Robert returned with the milk followed by a large woman who was Bernice's sister. They sat on either side of the bed while Genevieve sipped the milk. Robert soon wearied of waiting and excused himself from the room. Genevieve breathed a sigh of relief.

Bernice explained to her sister the situation and they all settled in for the delivery. As the contraction grew more frequent, Genevieve, though excited to meet her child, cried out in pain and wished it were all over.

After many hours, the baby managed to be delivered in spite of Genevieve's small frame. Exhausted and sweating, her hair matted, Genevieve was handed the small crying bundle. "You have a daughter! A little girl! She is rosy and strong! Listen to her cries! Congratulations!"

Genevieve wept with joy as she looked at her sweet daughter, Evechio's child! Her daughter already had wisps of dark hair. Is this what Evechio looked like as a baby? she wondered.

Robert was sent for as soon as Genevieve was fully ready. He raced into the room but his face fell when he heard it was a girl.

"I guess that will be nice for you, my dear, but I hope we can try for a boy?" was all he said.

Genevieve was too overjoyed to care about Robert's comment and was relieved when he soon left the room. The summer sun shone in the room and the smell of climbing roses drifted in with the breeze.

"Rose, that's what I'll call her. She is as sweet and pretty as a rose! Evechio used to bring me roses from the Medici gardens when he could. They would fill the room we lived in. Such sweet memories."

A shadow fell across her face as she thought how much sweeter this all would have been if he was here with them. But soon she was learning how to nurse the baby and then fell into a slumber with the baby in her arms.

Chapter Six

Rose grew to be a healthy, happy baby. Her eyes darkened until they were a deep brown, just like Evechio's. Her brown hair grew into delightful curls and her smile brightened the room. Robert showed little interest in her and then the day came that he questioned Genevieve about her.

"Rose doesn't look like you or me. I am blond and blue-eyed, you are a red-head with green eyes and there she is, a dark child. Why is this? I really have no feeling for her either. I just find babies to be distasteful and bothersome. And she is a girl, of no use! Perhaps we should send her away and start again." Robert said, coldly eyeing Rose as she sat in her mother's lap.

A mother's instinct rose up in Genevieve. "Don't you dare talk like that! She is my daughter, the joy of my life. If you want nothing to do with her, fine then just leave us alone or let us go to Florence!"

"Florence! Never! You are my wife and I want you by my side. But the child must go! I will find a convent that will take her."

Panic filled Genevieve. "You can't take her! She's my life, I would die!"

Before she knew what she was doing she yelled, "She's not even your child. You have no right!"

A deadly silence filled the room. Robert held his chest as if in pain and clutched his chair. Barely able to speak, he managed to get out, "She's not my child! She's not mine! Is she the child of the man you knew in Florence?! But you were my wife! How could you dare!"

In a rage, Robert rose and came towards them.

"Don't you dare touch us! If you do, I shall do everything in my power to leave you. I did it once and I can do it again!"

He paused in his rage, glaring at her. Coolly, she returned his gaze. As his rage dissipated, he stomped from the room.

The day passed without further confrontation much to Genevieve's relief. She knew that she would fight tooth and nail to keep Rose and that the time to return to Florence had come. But she also knew she had no means at all to go and with a baby in tow, she would never be able to make it. She would have to keep praying for some deliverance.

That night at their evening meal, Robert refused to look at her. They ate in silence and suddenly Robert got up and came to her. She shrank back in surprise as he grabbed her hand but she saw he had tears in his eyes.

"Please Genevieve, don't ever leave me again. I love you beyond bearing. But please let us try for a child of our own. If you do this, I will leave Rose to you. Can you live with that?"

Genevieve had been ready for a fight and was unprepared for Robert's sorrow. Her heart went out to him in his moment of need.

"Oh Robert, I'm sorry to see you so sad. If you really promise to leave Rose to me, yes, we can try for a child of our own."

He sank to his knees and covered her hand with kisses. Then he led her upstairs to his bed chamber with the hopes of conceiving a child.

Months went by and no child was conceived. Each night she had spent with Robert was torture to her. Invariably visions of his previous torments had come to her unbidden. His touch stiffened her immediately and she lay there in the bed unresponsive. Soon he tired of her and she was grateful for the respite.

One morning Genevieve woke with a start unsure of what to think. Her dream rested with her and awakened her heart. Many times, she had dreamed of Evechio but this dream was different. Her previous dreams took her to darkness and confusion. Evechio would drift in and out of the dreams, unsubstantial and distant. The dreams were more of a torment than a comfort.

But this dream was crystal clear, bright and colorful. Evechio stood in the monastery's garden praying. Yes, there was sorrow in his face but it changed to hope as he finished his prayer. Gently he leaned down and kissed a rose, caressing its petals. When he looked up, there were tears in his eyes.

Genevieve was overcome with emotion. Why was this dream so clear, so real? And of all the flowers in the garden, why did he choose a rose? Genevieve looked over at the cradle that held baby Rose. Did Evechio sense her existence? Genevieve felt huge excitement at the thought.

As Genevieve went through her day, she kept coming back to her dream. She wanted to call out Evechio's name and take him in her arms. She spent her day in a fantasy of being with him. The only thing that took her out of her reveries was baby Rose, the tending to her needs.

That night as she went to bed, Genevieve hoped to see Evechio in her dreams again. When she woke, she realized she had had the same dream! She lay in bed relishing its memory. The dream came back to her every night that week. Genevieve began to feel it was more than just a mere dream; it was a message!

The urgency to know the answer consumed her. She sat down at her desk and wrote a letter to St. Grief. She asked if Evechio was there and to tell him she was alive and well. She smuggled the letter to the stables and begged one of the grooms to take it to be delivered.

She could barely contain her excitement. She sang, she danced, her step was light, her smile broad. Thankfully Robert seemed oblivious. She sang to Rose and twirled her in the air.

"My little Rose, you will love your Papa, he is such a gentle loving soul."

Chapter Seven

G enevieve wondered how long it would take to get a response. She tried to contain her excitement and avoided Robert as much as possible. Sunday came and off to church she went full of grateful prayers. When she went to confession, she was eager to tell Pere LeMaitre.

"Mon Pere," she began but before she could continue, the screen that separated them opened and a letter appeared.

"Genevieve, this letter arrived from St. Grief for you. I was told you should receive it in secret. I hope all is well with you and the baby."

Before he had finished, Genevieve had already torn open the letter and unfolded it. It held two simple sentences:

"I love you. I'm coming."

Genevieve's soul soared with joy. He was alive and well and she would see him again! They would be reunited!

"All is perfect, Mon Pere. God has answered my prayers," she said.

Full of excitement, she spent her day imagining their reunion and planning her release from Robert. This time would be different, she wouldn't run in fear, she would walk away strong and proud. She would face Robert head on.

The next morning, she went to the main hall to find Robert. She was no longer the frightened child he had wed and abused. She was the mother of a child and a woman profoundly in love. And Robert was not the same man. Since he had stopped drinking and his gambling ways, he was a better man, just not a man she could ever love. She hoped for the best.

"Robert, I must speak with you about something of huge importance."

"Yes Dear, what do you want?" he said with a smile.

She knew this would be hard and his smile disarmed her. But it was necessary. Yes, she was about to hurt Robert deeply but she had to think of Evechio and Rose to give her courage. "You and I have had a troubled past. You know I don't love you and never could. It has been two years and nothing in my heart has changed. I am still plagued my memories of your brutality every time you touch me. We are just beyond the point of reconciliation. You are my husband in name only. Please, I beg of you. Give me my freedom!"

Robert's face paled and his mouth worked wordlessly. Finally he was able to stutter: "Have you gone mad? You are my wife! We are a family!"

"But Rose is not even your child. As well, you are indifferent to her because she is not a boy and therefore not worthy of being your heir. And we have tried for a child without success."

"But even if I let you go, how would you live? Have you thought of that?!" The moment of truth had arrived.

"I have been in touch with Evechio. He is coming for us whether you are ready to let me go or not."

Robert's stricken face became infused with anger.

"Evechio!?! How does he dare come here to my home to take my wife! Is he mad? I will not let him near you!" Robert yelled trembling with rage.

There was a time when Genevieve would have been filled with fear at Robert's rage but she had been young and alone. Now she was a mother and had Evechio's love to bolster her. She did not cower or run from his rage. She knew she would fight back this time if she had too.

"Robert, I'm not afraid of you anymore and I won't change my mind. We can part friends or enemies, it's up to you. And how can you wish to hold onto such a sham of a marriage? Don't you want a chance to love and be loved in return? A chance to have children of your own? Don't you see how much better this will be for both of us?"

She put her hand on his arm and the rage drained out of him. Robert sat down and put his face in his hands. His shoulders sank and he began to sob.

"But why, why can't you love me? That's all I've ever wanted from the day we met. I'm a different man now. I thought you had forgiven me."

He turned his tear-stained face to her and she felt her heart leap with pity.

"Robert, I know you are a different man. I have forgiven you but I can't forget. Every time you touch me, the memories come flooding back. Do you really want me to live like that? If you really do care, you would want me to be happy."

She put her hand on his shoulder and his face showed resignation. Yes, she thought, he is a different man and I might have loved him but for our tortured past.

She caressed his weathered face, kissed his forehead and said "Good bye. You will always be my friend."

Elated, she knew she had won.

Genevieve spent the day in her room with Rose, packing the things she would need in her new life. Rose napped and when awake, played with her dollies. Genevieve felt so blessed to have such a good-natured baby and she couldn't wait to show her to Evechio.

When she was done, Genevieve sat by the window waiting for the sound of a carriage. The sun shone as if reflecting her mood. As the sun was setting and the last rays of light illuminated the grounds, she heard it. The crunch of wheels on the drive was unmistakable.

Gathering Rose up in her arms, she raced down the hall and stairs to the entrance hall. She flew passed Robert as he emerged from the great hall, and rushed out the door. There stood Evechio with open arms, as handsome as ever, just as Genevieve remembered him.

She rushed to his embrace smelling deeply the warm familiar scent of his body. Showering her with kisses, he pulled her from him to look her in the eyes. Tears streamed down both their faces.

"Evechio, you have to meet Rose, my daughter! I mean, our daughter!!!" Evechio looked at Rose with her deep brown eyes and brown curls.

"Is she…, is she really mine? I mean ours?!"

He kissed her on the forehead and wrapped them both in his arms again.